S0-AEB-757

NOON

NOON is an independent not-for-profit literary annual published by NOON, Inc.

Edition price $9.00 (domestic) or $14.00 (foreign)
All donations are tax deductible.

NOON is distributed by
Ingram Periodicals, Inc., 1240 Heil Quaker Boulevard,
LaVergne, Tennessee 37086 (800) 627-6247 and

Bernhard DeBoer, Inc., 113 East Centre Street,
Nutley, New Jersey 07110 (973) 667-9300

NOON welcomes submissions. Send to:

Diane Williams
NOON 1369 Madison Avenue PMB 298 New York New York 10128
Please include the necessary self-addressed, stamped envelope.

ISSN 1526-8055
ISBN 0-9676211-4-3

Printed in U.S.A.

CONTENTS

"Look, the real reason I'm coming is you."

JANE AND THE CANE

LYDIA DAVIS

Mother could not find her cane. She had a cane, but she could not find her special cane. Her special cane had a handle that was the head of a dog. Then she remembered: Jane had her cane. Jane had come to visit. Jane had needed a cane to get back home. That was two years ago. Mother called Jane. She told Jane she needed her cane. Jane came with a cane. When Jane came, Mother was tired and lying in bed. She did not look at the cane. Jane left and went back home. Mother got out of bed and looked at the cane. Then she saw that it was not the same cane. It was a plain cane. She called Jane and told her it was not the same cane. But Jane was tired. She was too tired to talk, she said. She was going to bed.

The next morning she came with the cane. Mother got out of bed. She looked at the cane. It was the right cane. It had the head of a dog on it, the head of a sort of spaniel, brown and white. Jane went home with the other cane, the plain cane. After Jane was gone, Mother complained, she complained on the phone: why did Jane not bring back the cane? Why did Jane bring the wrong cane? Mother was tired. Oh, Mother was so tired of Jane and the cane.

THE GOOD TASTE CONTEST

LYDIA DAVIS

The husband and wife were competing in a Good Taste Contest judged by a jury of their peers, men and women of good taste including a fabric designer, a rare book dealer, a pastry cook, and a librarian. The wife was judged to have better taste in furniture, especially antique furniture. The husband was judged to have overall poor taste in lighting fixtures, tableware, and glassware. The wife was judged to have indifferent taste in window treatments but the husband and wife both were judged to have good taste in floor coverings, bed linen, bath linen, large appliances, and small appliances. The husband was felt to have good taste in carpets, but only fair taste in upholstery fabrics. The husband was felt to have very good taste in both food and alcoholic beverages, while the wife had inconsistently good to poor taste in food. The husband had better taste in clothes than the wife though inconsistent taste in perfumes and colognes. While both husband and wife were judged to have no more than fair taste in garden design, they were judged to have good taste in number and variety of evergreens. The husband was felt to have excellent taste in roses but poor taste in bulbs. The wife was felt to have better taste in bulbs and generally good taste in shade plantings with the exception of hostas. The husband's taste was felt to be good in garden furniture, but only fair in ornamental planters. The wife's taste was judged consistently poor in garden statuary. After a brief discussion, the judges gave the decision to the husband for his higher overall points score.

BEGIN WITH TEMPER

ADAM PHILLIPS

I

I remember it as a calm time, as calmness goes. The stretcher was never used. I was positively skittish, so much so that I asked Edith for the photograph of the chandelier. I pored over it. You can picture me, I expect, all ears for the past, putting the old ballroom through its paces, the walls lavender . . . such a feast in black and white, the floor shiny from its shoes . . . scuffs I am told polish over time, which is a lifeline of a thought if ever there was one . . . and the ladies as they were then called, for short but not for long, gorgeous in their gowns, everyone up and about and more than game. As a younger man, I should say, I was unusually understated. I wasn't given, let us say, to . . . I was not the kind of youth who would intrigue people with his good manners, as the ladies were so good at doing I have noticed. The advantage of being nothing special is that it is so easy to keep up. There was no more to me because I proffered no incentives. I was ablaze with anonymity then . . . I had my frustrations, I want to be quite clear about that, as my dear father used to say, and as wants go it is indeed unexceptionable, I had my frustrations, my voracious boredoms, my dark nights of what I can't call . . . I was disarmed by the nights. In my dreams I was impressed by the things we are impressed by, though it occurs to me now that I was never out of my depth, whatever that might mean . . . I was in my depth, such as it was. I saw things . . . I needed other people . . . other people have always reassured me that things weren't true, a blessing in its way, though as I was saying, a little understated. But I was calm enough for once to ask Edith for the photograph and it would be foolhardy at this stage to regret it . . . there are regrets, I hasten to add, that I would be prepared to confess to . . . to confess to myself, but that is for another chapter. The suspense will not kill us.

II

Perhaps an example would be in order? A person I will call, for the sake of confidentiality, Edith, and myself, whom I will call nothing for the same reason, are making love in a hotel bedroom in, let us say, Lisbon . . . I don't remember, but the country, as you will see, is hardly the point of the story. At one point I say to Edith, turn over on your front. And she replies, which is my front? That's what I mean when I say that the introduction is never foolproof. That a man may smile and smile and just be. There is an atmosphere for every occasion and we don't always get it right! As I say, I could only start once the introductions were over. It was bombast, if that is still a word. I was never encouraged . . . extravagance comes to mind . . . I was not a person for entering a room. I had no examples. I had no vocation for others . . . all my inclinations were in the other direction, away from the company, though my appetite for songs is undimmed to this day. The sentimental crosses my mind. Romance was never too much fuss for me and it was ever thus. I did the usual things. I took exception to being ignored. I tried my fears. I made the necessary passes, as they were then called. But in those days, I believe, we were all distracted. Too blank to be brave. We approached each other, and not only approached, with too little in mind. There was a torque of fantasy, of commentary, everything came with too much topping. Perhaps we didn't talk out loud enough to ourselves when we were alone. Perhaps we just had the wrong memories. We will never know. But the overhearing theme and it didn't seem to matter who referred to it, was always too portentous. Well, too portentous for us at least, and there wasn't anyone else as far as we could see.

III

I'm cramming, I know, but what else can one do in a maze? I feel a tightening of the pipes when I talk about this. Of course, there were always allusions that I missed, tantrums that I forbade myself at point of death, excuses that turned into prophecies. That I could take for granted. As a boy I would watch the birds through the window stabbing the lawn. I obviously stayed put, they obviously would come and go, hearing things presumably. But I was never torn, I never went silly and started saying yes to the birds. Which is why I adore the chandelier . . . fond is not a good word, though I use it a lot as I get older, I find . . . though I would be pushed to say why . . . fit to fit is the phrase that comes to mind . . . Anyway, it is temper we should be talking of, what we are tempered by, all the words that begin with temper. Temper, temper as they used to say, when conjuring.

HAUNT OF JACKALS

DAMIEN OBER

One one one one one one one one one one one one one one one. One one one one one one one one one one one one one one one one one one one one one one one one one one one one one one one one one. One one one one one one one one one one one one one one one one one one one one one one one one one one one one one one one one one one one one one one one one one one one one one one one one one. One one one one one one one one one one.

One one one one one one one one one one. One one one one one. One one one one one one one one one one one one one one one one one one one one one one one one one one one one one one one one one one one one one. One one one one. One one one one one one.

One one one one one one one one one one one one one one one. One one one one one one one one one one one one one one one one one one one one one one one one one one one one one one one one. One one one one one.

One one one one one, one one one one one, one one one one one one one. One one one one one one one one. One one one one one one one one one one, "One one one."

"One, one one one one," one one one one one one, "One one one."

One one one one one. One one one. One one one one one, "One one one one." One one.

One one one one one one one one—one one one one. One one one one one one one one one, one one one one one one one one one, one one, one one one one one one one one one one. One one one one one one one.

One one one one one one one one, one one. One one one one one. One one one one one one one one one one one one one one one one one one one one one one one one one one one one one one one one one one one one one one one one one one one one one one one one. One, one one one one one one one one one one one one one one one one one one one one one. One one one one one one one one one one one one one one one one one one one one one one one one? One one one.

"One one one one one one one one," one one.

"One one one," one one one one one, "one."

"One one one?"

One one one one, one one one one, one one one, one one,

"One one one."

One one one one one one one, one one one one one one one.

One one one one one one one one, one one one one, one one one one one one. One one one one one one one. One one *one* one one one one one one one. One one one one one one one. One one one one. One one one one one one. One one, one one one-one one one one. One one one one. One one one, one. One one one one one one.

One one one one one one one one one one one one, one one one one one one, one one one one. One one one one. One one one one one. One one one one one, one one one one one one-one one one one. One one one one one one one one, one, one, one, one one one one. One one one one one one, one one one one one one. One one. One one one one one one. One.

One.

One one one one one one one one one one, one one one one. One one one one one one one. One one one one one one one one. One one.

One one one one one one one one one one one one one one one one one one one one one one one one one one one one, one one one one one one one one one one one one one one one one one one one one one one one one one one one one one one one one one one one one one one one one one one one one one one one one. One one one one one. One one one one one. One one one one. One one one one one one one one one one one one one one.

One one one one one one one one, one one one one one, one-one one, one one one one one one one. One one, one, one, one one one one one one. One one one one one one one one one one—one one one one one one one, one, one one.

One one one one one one one, one one. One one, "One one one one one."

One one one.

"One, one one one one one?"

"One one one," one one one-one one.

One one one one one one. One one. One one one one one, one one one one, one one one one. One one one one one one. "One one one one one?"

One one, one one one, one one, "One one one one," one one one one, "one one one one one one."

One one one one one one one one. One one.

"One one one one one," one one one one one one. "One one one one one one."

One one one one one one one one one. One one one one.

One one one one one. One one one.

"One one one one, one one," one one one one one one one one one.

One one one one one one. One one one one one, one one one one one, one one one one one.

One one one one one one one one one. One one one one one one one one one one one one one one one one one one one one one

one one one one one. One one one—one one one one one one, one one, one one one, one one one one, one one one one one. One one one one. One one one one one one one. One one one. One one one one one one one one one one. One, one one one one, one one one one one one one one. One one one one one one, *one one one one one one one*. One one one one one one one, one one one one, one one one one. One one one one one.

One one one one one one one one one. One one one one one, one, one one one one one one one. One one one one one. One one, one one one one one one one, one one one one one one. One one one one one one one. One one one one one one one one one one one one one one one one one one one one one one one one one one one one one one one one one one one one one. One one one one one one one one one one one one one one one one one one one one one one one one one.

One one one one one one one one one one one one one one one one one one one one one one one one one one. One one one one one one one; one one one one one one. One one one one one one one, one one one. One one one one one one one. One one one one, one one one one one one.

“One one one one one one one one one, one one,” one one, one. One one one one one one one.

“One one one one one one.”

“One,” one one one, one one one one one. One one one one one, one one one one one one one one one one.

One one one one one. One one one one one. One one one. One one, one one one one one one one one one. One one one one

one one one one one one one one one one one one one one one one one one one one one one one one one one one one one one one one one one one one one one one one one one. One one one one one one one one one one one one one one one one one one one one. One one one one one one one one one one one. One one one one one one one one one one one. One one one one one one one.

One one one one one one one one one one one one one one one one one one one one one one one one one one. One one one one one. One one one one, one one one.

“One one one one one,” one one one. “One one one one one.”

One one, “One,” one one one one, one one one, “one one one one one one, one.”

THE LITTLE FUCKERS

KARL ROLOFF

We were by no means taking this shit lightly. I rassled with her daily, and every time she hurt herself I got sympathy pains. I could always count on her to make me feel better. We had a fucking stockpile of experiences together that totally prepared us.

It was decided that we would wait until the week until after homecoming, because I had a collage that I was making out of macaroni that required my undivided attention. I decided that I would practice by masturbating and watching myself in the mirror, so I could get the expression on my face down right. I had to look like I had every right to this vagina. And she practiced sexy porn faces she had researched on the Internet. That's fucking hot, and she was completely willing to do that. So it was clearly going to be good fucking sex. I know that putting my dick in Cindy is going to feel better than with just some random girl. Because with Cindy it's making love. It's not the moistness of the vagina, it's the person who has the vagina that counts.

A week before it happened I found her in her room crying on the floor with pictures from her childhood scattered all around the room. I asked her what was wrong.

"You don't understand. Once we do this everything will be different. We have to change, and we have to say good-bye to this, to all this."

"Why? You really liked childhood that much?"

"Yes. Yes," she said, sniffling.

I was puzzled about how to respond. I didn't know why she liked her childhood so much. I thought about my own childhood for a second but it really didn't seem very important to me. "The only thing I really remember about my childhood is that there were a lot of bugs. Bugs fucking everywhere, you couldn't step on the little fuckers fast enough, they just kept coming back." Yeah, bugs. Huh. I became lost in the memory. "Yeah. That's the only thing I can really remember."

She didn't quite understand this. "What, did you guys have like an ant or roach problem or something?"

"No, I can't say that we did." That's true. *Why the fuck am I* thinking about bugs, here? I suddenly became very confused about something that had made complete sense a few moments ago. "To tell you the truth I have no fucking idea where they came from. Just everywhere, bugs."

I explained to her the best thing to do about this was to not think about it, and any other problem that ever came up in reference to this or anything else ever, that the best policy was to just fucking pretend that it wasn't going on. If you think about things long and hard enough, you'll realize that thinking never helps. And Cindy had thought herself into a corner. Things have a real capacity to not exist if you can't handle them at all.

Then the big day came! I was so excited I blew my load in my sleep, in the shower, at breakfast, in homeroom, and near a bookstore. I had to fucking haul ass to make it to her house before I blew my load again.

I got to the door and Cindy answered.

I was out of breath. "Huh, huh, quick! Quick, open—open up your pussy!" I yelled. I took my cock out and tried to put it up into her, but it was too late. I sprayed her door frame like a lion marking his territory. "Fuck, I'm sorry!" I yelled, leaning up against the door in exhaustion.

We got into her room and Cindy shut the door. I blew a load on her rug. I was just really excited. Cindy took off her jeans, and I took off my jeans. I took off her shirt and my shirt. She took off her panties, and I took off my underwear. We stood looking at each other. She didn't look as good as she did with her clothes on. She had little pockets of fat that graced her otherwise perfect features, and these little imperfections had been well concealed under her clothes. When she had her clothes on, and she walked around talking to people in the world and doing things, she looked somehow different. Now it was like she was being insensitive to me even though she wasn't saying anything. It was like she had been drained of everything that got us to this point.

She stared at my dick. She had never really seen it before, at least not with so much ceremony. She must have been impressed because she had absolutely no reaction.

"Fuck me," she said, sticking her pinky into her mouth.

Shit, that was all I needed to hear. I jumped on her.

"Okay, put it in slow. Slowly."

It felt great! I had never felt anything so wonderful. I felt so comfortable and so opened up into something new, something that was truly different.

"Not too hard. Gentle."

I had never felt such a feeling. I was putting myself into everything that now mattered. I would walk differently now, I would have a different expression on my face. My love for Cindy was different, now. I could touch it, and I could feel myself poking inside of it. I loved her so much. I had never loved her so much.

"I love you," I said.

"Hey, can we stop for a second?"

I held onto her hand. She squeezed my hand so hard I thought it was going to burst. I felt my eyes fill with tears.

"Ouch! Please, can we just stop."

Finally, I blew my load for real. Right inside of her as she yelled along with me. I'll never be able to describe the feeling. Everything meant everything for a moment, and then the moment completely ended.

I fell over on top of her. I pulled out my dick. I felt as if something terribly wrong had just taken place. And now Cindy was sad about something and I would have to fucking fix it for her. I put my head in my hands so that I could pretend to be by myself with no one to comfort me.

BOAT

DEB OLIN UNFERTH

Go to the hotel, they said and pointed. She did not want to go to that hotel. It was a mess of rebar and rotted wood.

Where's the best hotel in town? Ms. Green said. She swept her hand over the line of shacks, the mud hills beyond.

This one's cheap, they said.

No, she wants the best.

Oh, there's a very nice one, but it's expensive, they said. They nodded and shook their heads. It's so expensive, so expensive. You better not go there.

I don't care about the cost, she said. I'll pay anything.

Anything, they said. She'll pay anything. Where's Nico? they said. Nico walked over with his wild limp. He was young and perfectly formed and shining. He scooped up Ms. Green and put her in a shopping cart. He wheeled her away. The town lined up to watch as he bumped her down the rock road. Everyone cheered.

The hotel was six dollars a night and instead of a shower had a barrel of water which wasn't too bad as far as these things go. She ventured out to find a phone. She was spending most of her money on calls to the States to see if her boyfriend, wherever he was, had left her a message.

Does anyone have a phone in this town? she said.

I'll pay anyone with a phone, she said.

Come with me, said a boy. They walked on planks of wood thrown across the mud. They stood on a porch and called into the dark, *Desculpe? Hay teléfono?* A woman shook her head sadly, *No, no hay teléfono.* They went everywhere—to the school, which was closed, to the office of ships, to another office whose light drifted back and forth with alarm. Her escort introduced her grandly. She is going to Bluefields. She must find a phone. Her grandmother is sick. Her husband worried. Her boss apoplectic. He spoke long and eloquently. He used his hands to express his humility, her desire, his duty. They walked back on a road as blue as Bluefields in dreams.

She had no messages.

In the morning she and the others assembled for the *panga*. People had arrived in the night on a boat, or a bus, or a horse, or a cart. Now there was one space left and they sat in their life jackets waiting. The sun was an unfriendly arrow. Finally three people came walking down the dock with their boxes and nets and suitcases. To Bluefields? they said. Bluefields?

Nobody knew what to do.

At last they had to admit they were going there, too. And everyone took off their life jackets and climbed out of the *panga*, one by one, and walked across the dock to a bigger *panga* and put on other life jackets and sat back down. Everything was fine. Until the man who owned the first *panga* came walking over in a slouch.

It was all right with him. His feelings weren't hurt. He didn't mind if they wanted to take the other man's *panga*. Even if he had bought the gas. Even if he had sat with them for hours one day and hours another. He didn't mind. But no way was anybody getting their money back.

Ms. Green wanted to say, Oh, for God's sake, fine, let's all pay again, but she certainly knew better than to say that. So they all took off their life jackets and lined off the bigger *panga* and got back on the smaller *panga* and put back on the other life jackets and sat back down. Somehow they managed to squeeze all three of those men on, too.

And then the man said, We can't go on, the boat is sinking. And indeed it was, water spilling over the sides. Two of the three men climbed out of the *panga* and stood on the dock with their luggage in a pile beside them. The town spired behind them. And then the *panga* was off.

They kept telling Ms. Green to sit in the middle. Women in the middle, they said, but she wouldn't budge. She wanted to look at the jungle as they passed or some such thing, but as soon as they started going she could see why women sat in the middle. The water rose around them and sprayed into the boat and then it began to rain and everybody at once pulled a giant piece of plastic over the boat which the people not in the middle had to hold down with their fingers. Which with the wind it was very hard to hold. Ms. Green's side kept flying up and everyone yelled at her and finally they made her crawl over someone and get in the middle like they said in the first place.

Then the luggage flew off the boat and into the water. Huge boxes, which broke when they hit the surface and clothes went everywhere. Rain poured out of the sky like in the days of Noah, but they had to pull off the plastic and go back and lean over into the water and fish the clothes out of the river and put them, mud-heavy, in the boat between their legs.

But they did finally arrive.

And now the question was: why did Ms. Green go to Bluefields? Certainly she didn't remember the original secret reason, as she walked from the dock, nor the purported reason, the one she explained to people over and over. The most recent reason, the one reason that had propelled her forward each dawn, was that she thought she would find tourists at the other end. She thought she would find bank machines and beaches and blue skies and song. Bring on the Caribbean dream. Why did she think that? Who other than she would come this far and go this long? Who other than she? She walked from the dock, numb-wet, wanting only a phone. The main street was a pit of mud.

Come to think of it, she left the first place to get away from the blue skies and bank machines.

And the first place was where?

Who knows. There have been plenty of firsts.

A year later she was in another country, far from the brown waters of Blue. It seems impossible that she could still be waiting for her boyfriend to call but she was: a different boyfriend or maybe the same one with a different name. Maybe there was no boyfriend anymore, only the habit of phone calls home. That feeling is so familiar, it may be all there is to her.

She was staying in the Hotel Caribbean Dream, of all things, for four dollars a night. A man said the word "Bluefields" to her as if it were a question and she sat down and told them what she knew—the *panga,* the rain, the roads like gunshots.

That's not much, someone said suddenly. His face emerged from behind a T-shirt—the room doubled as a laundry and dine-in. Clothes hung on lines down the room. He said, That's not much, which she didn't think was very friendly.

Not much? said someone else. I suppose it could have been worse if she drowned.

So at least someone was on her side. But if they wanted to hear the worst, she could have told them. And she knows the worst because she heard it in Bluefields.

That first day in Bluefields, she didn't see any tourists like she'd hoped. A truck like a tank wobbled down the street and sprinkled a great mist of repellent over them all. The earth rumbled with a minor quake and everyone held out their hands for balance. But then she came out of her hotel and saw a North American sitting on a step as if he were in Brooklyn.

I haven't seen anyone like me in a week, said Ms. Green.

A week? he said. Who's like you? There's no part of that sentence I understand.

Where are the tourists, she said, the reggae bars?

I've never seen a tourist here, he said. He studied her. Is that what you are?

No, she said. I'm looking for a phone.

And lo and behold he and Ms. Green were from the same town although he didn't know how to act like someone from that town anymore. He kept trying to pay for her Cokes.

In the U.S. women pay for themselves these days, she thought it fair to inform him.

Is that right? he said.

And lo and behold he knew just where to find a phone. As they walked through the streets to reach it he said, I have a girlfriend, a local, just so you know.

I have a boyfriend, she said.

(She wasn't sure of that.)

Oh yeah, a boyfriend, he said. Just be careful. I don't want mine to do any voodoo on you.

She had no messages.

It was on a hill they walked up that he told her what happened, the worst she ever heard. They walked up that hill in the heat and the drizzle for the same reason people ride rivers or sail out into the sea.

I was fishing off the coast of Bluefields, he said. I had a crew of three. I was standing on the deck, looking out at the water. Suddenly they jumped on me, three at once, and hit me over the head with a pipe.

A pirate ship! gasped Ms. Green.

Not a pirate ship, he said a little annoyed. It was my ship.

They jumped on me, he said. One was hitting my legs with the pipe and another was hitting my head. Blood everywhere. I wouldn't go down.

Why not? she gasped.

I was screaming, I was crazy. I don't know what I was doing. I went down at last. They tied me up with cord. Look, I have scars still. Look at my ankles. Still I limp from the pipe.

He still had scars around his ankles—thick, uneven rings.

They held a machete to my throat, he said. You're going to fucking die, man, die in Bluefields, one kept saying.

Let me do him right now, another kept saying. I've got to do him. Then they locked me in a room and left me there. I pushed the air conditioner out the window and jumped into the water. I escaped.

He and Ms. Green walked down to the Bluefields dock. It was dusk and a hundred years' worth of birds were flying in, coming over the rooftops. They landed and landed on wires, on posts. Still more arrived and more, circling in from all sides. They were strikes, clouds. The noise was an invasion, the air was a long note. It cannot be described on a page. It would be impossible to capture in a movie. There is no way to represent it. Being there wouldn't do it. You'd have to *be Ms. Green*, see what she saw. It was like an emergency, like she had stopped breathing, the first bell toll of the apocalypse.

Meanwhile men chopped their coconut.

I'd like to go home, he said. Are you like most people at home?

Ms. Green is like most people at home.

It was freezing in that water, he said. And shark-infested. I was bleeding. I was so far from land. I swam for hours. At last I made it and crawled up on the rocks. I ran to a door, a long trail of blood behind me. I pounded on the door and an old man opened it. I told him, I'll give you five hundred dollars cash. I'll go to the bank and give you five hundred dollars cash if you'll drive me in your boat to the U.S. military base right now.

You said that? she gasped.

Well, first I asked him for a glass of water. I was immensely thirsty. Can I have a glass of water? I said, and then I said I'd give him five hundred bucks. The old man said, Five hundred U.S. dollars? All right, let's go! And we went out to his boat but the damn thing wouldn't start. He kept trying, and finally I said, Old man, give me that thing, and I nearly tore the engine off.

What happened to the engine? she said.

I started it and I was saved, he said.

JUAN THE CELL PHONE SALESMAN

DEB OLIN UNFERTH

It was a holiday which means the woman in question went home. And this included an encounter with the mother of the woman in question, and the mother's questioning of the woman upon her arrival. The woman questioned waited for her special box on the go-round and endured.

That same evening, over chicken and lemonade, the mother made a strange statement: she had pinpointed on this earth the Perfect Man for the woman in question. Actually she had found two. But one perfect man was out of town so luckily there was another.

The second Perfect Man had a name and a career and those were Juan and cellular phone salesman respectively. The mother and the little sister showed the woman the phone he had touched and sold them and explained how its presence had transformed them into a super-efficient mother/daughter tag team. Team of two, that is, until today, happily, now three, if only momentarily, now that she, older sister, woman in question, was home.

A cell phone salesman, said the woman. This is who you want your daughter to plan her future with.

How, said the mother, did my daughter come to be such a snob.

The woman questioned was slipping through thin fingers as she phoned Juan the cellular phone salesman on mother's cellular phone, phone to phone, phoned because when the woman at first refused, mother said that she was deliberately ruining Christmas for everyone.

Several hours if not a whole day had elapsed by this time. And then there were several more hours, if not a whole day, while the woman and mother and sister waited for Juan to pick up his cellular and phone their home. Which he didn't. The mother carried the cellular phone from room to room, set it next to her as she pinned balls to the tree, and said, Where is he? Where could he be? Maybe she should call again. How did she know he'd even gotten the message, those cell phones are so unreliable and she should call again.

Obediently, foolishly, the woman in question did call again, while meeting eyes with the younger sister and noting a note of sympathy in them because everyone knows that according to the social rules and regulations we have agreed on, to leave two messages for a stranger is a bit untoward. But she left it, then retreated to her bedroom like the old days.

Sure enough, he still didn't call, and sure enough, the mother was like a bride left at the altar. How dare he not call. She walked through the house, checking the phones one by one. He had said he'd like to take her out and she had shown him the nicest picture and now why would he lie, the bastard. Slowly, slowly, the mother circled around and around with the cellular phone. She tried to be casual, the mother, tapping on the door, Hey, let's call Juan! like it was a forgotten invitation to a party. But the woman—woman, yes, not a little girl of nine—would not be fooled and even the sister agreed that three times was two times too many but when the mother began to get the swirled crazy eyes, the woman grabbed the phone and phoned again. This time though she lost all patience and dignity and said onto his voice mail the devastating: Hello Juan, my mother would like to go out with you.

What happened next happened fast, which is why the mistake about the off button was made. When mother grabbed the phone from the woman, she screamed a word that wasn't very nice about the woman in question, screamed it before she realized about the off button, that nobody had pressed it, and everybody stood horrified for one long moment before mother ran from the room.

That afternoon the sister and the woman in question had fun with the phone, shouting desperately into the cellular, *Juan, we miss you, Juan!* or sternly, *Juan, you're ruining Christmas for everyone*, or sadly, *Juan, please call us, Juan, and leave us a little message*, or angrily, *It's over for good this time, Juan. Don't ever call us again!* And the woman in question felt, well, pleased with her sister, but also a bit unwomanly as she stuck herself under her thin blanket that evening.

This part is miraculous: Juan phoned the next day. He phoned while the woman was showering.

He phoned and I nearly dropped the receiver, said the sister, which would not have been good. These little phones are delicate creatures.

He phoned and he spoke charmingly, said the sister. He, as always, asked many interesting questions.

Which is impossible, of course, to even say such a thing because how long is always if you've only spoken to him twice?

It's the kind of man he is, insisted the sister. The kind who asks questions and listens and asks more questions.

Like a talk show host, said the woman. What a treat. Still she will go out with him on this very night. And for the next several hours the three, they are a three, yes. Look at them, they sew and unclutter, they pin hair and dresses. How womanly they are, how sisterly, how motherly, daughterly.

And now here is the climax. Look how they stand in the mirror, the three, and joke and apply lipstick for the Coming Juan, the cell phone salesman. The sister says she almost wishes she could go in her place and the woman in question says she doesn't see why she shouldn't, who cares if she's only sixteen, the sister and she could simply swap names. Or better yet they could both go and say they have the same name and are, in fact, doubles. And the sister and the woman practice in the mirror saying her name over and over, in unison and separately, and the mother joins in like a song. This is a nice moment.

The next moment is not so nice. It will be a few hours later and Juan will be very drunk and unable to drive the woman in question home. She will also be drunk and having an unpleasant time with Juan who can be a little mean. And she will—by this time she is in his apartment, an unsavory detail—phone mother on Juan's cellular phone at three in the morning, and mother and sister will come to retrieve her, minus one shoe which she will never recover, and it will be at this moment that Juan will utter the only statement anyone anywhere will ever remember him making, and he will roar it as he lifts his head from between two couch cushions: "Get your drunk sister out of here!" he will say and that will be his great contribution. Thank you, Juan.

The very last part is this: We are in the front seat without any lipstick on, me and mother and sister. It is dark and late. We aren't talking about Juan.

CHRISTOPHER WILLIAMS

PHOTOGRAPHS

UOU 087

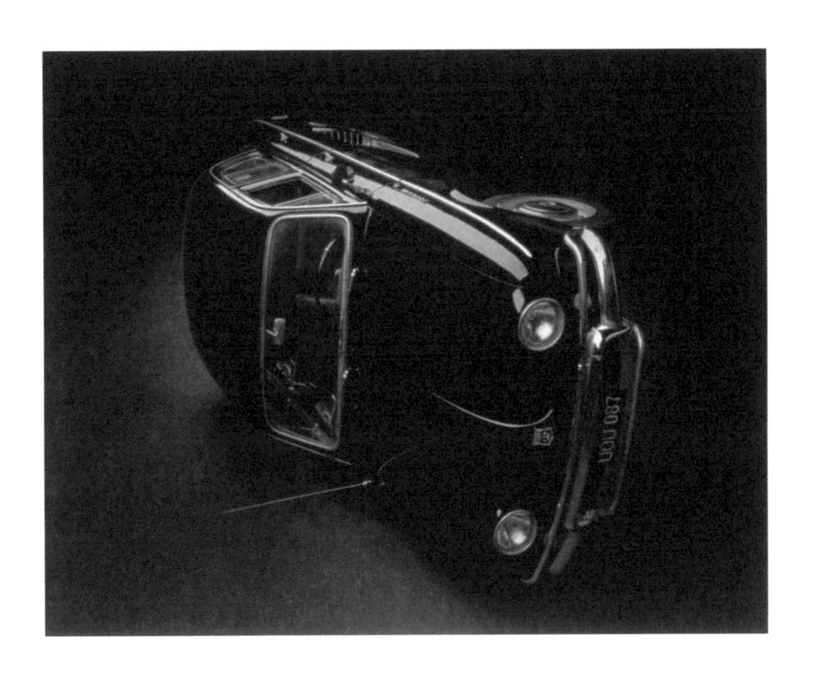
UOU 087

UOU 087

UOU 087

UOU 087

Model: 1964 Renault Dauphine-Four, R 1095
Body Type & Seating: 4-dr sedan – 4 to 5 persons
Engine Type: 14/52 Weight : 1397 lbs
Price: $1495,00 USD (original)
ENGINE DATA:
Base four: inline, overhead-value four cylinder
Cast iron block and aluminum head W/removable cylinder sleeves
Displacement: 51.5 cu. in. (845 oc.)
Bore and Stroke: 2.28x3.15 in. (58 x 80 mm)
Compression Ratio: 7.25:1
Brake Horsepower: 32 (SAE) at 4200 rpm
Torque: 50lbs At 2000 rpm, Three main bearings
Solid valve lifters
Single downdraft carburetor
CHASSIS DATA:
Wheelbase: 89 in. Overall length: 155 in. Height: 57 in.
Width: 60 in. Front thread: 49 in. Rear thread: 48 in.
Standard Tires: 5.50 x 15 in.
TECHNICAL:
Layout: rear engine, rear drive
Transmission: four speed manual
Steering: rack and pinion
Suspension
(front): independent coil springs Suspension
(back): independent with swing axles and coil springs
Brakes: front/rear disc
Body construction: steel unibody
PRODUCTION DATA:
Sales: 18,432 sold in U.S. in 1964 (all types)
Manufacturer: Regie Nationale des Usines
Renault, Billancourt, France
Distributor: Renault Inc., New York, NY., U.S.A.
Serial number: R-10950059799
Engine Number: Type 670-05 # 191563
California License Plate number: UOU 087
Vehicle ID Number: 0059799
Los Angeles, California
January 15, 2000
2000
Gelatin silver print
11 x 14 inches
28 x 35.5 cm
(Numbers 1-11)

A HAPPY RURAL SEAT OF VARIOUS VIEW: LUCINDA'S GARDEN

CHRISTINE SCHUTT

They met Gordon Brisk on a Friday the thirteenth at the Bay View in Brooksville. They pooh-poohed the ominous signs. The milky stew they ate was cold—so what? They were happy. They were at sea; they were at the mess, corkskinned roughs in rummy spirits, dumb, loud, happy. And they really didn't have so much to say to each other. They were only a few months married and agreed on everything, and for the moment nearly everything they did—where and how they lived—was cheap or free. They expected gifts at every turn and got them.

So it was at the Bay View on a Friday night—lime pits along the rim of the glass, Pie feeling puckered—when Gordon Brisk introduced himself as a friend of Aunt Lucinda's from a long time ago. Nick said he had seen Gordon's paintings, of course. And

Gordon said, "I'm not surprised."

Gordon told a story that included Aunt Lucinda when she was their age, young. There were matches in it and another young woman who almost died. Aunt Lucinda in the story was the same —all love, love, love and this time for Gordon—and as for Gordon himself? He held up us his hands. His hands had been on fire. He said, "Just look at these fuckers," and they did. They looked and looked. The hands should have scared them, but they were drunk and sunburned and happy. They were glad, they insisted, glad to have met him. "Our first famous person," Pie said after the after-dinner drinks when she and Nick were in the Crosley driving home.

Pie was driving, too fast; she was saying how she loved those amber-colored, oversweet drinks, the ones floated with an orange slice and a cherry. She had had too many, so was it any surprise she hit something? She hit what they thought was a raccoon. It was definitely something large and dark, but fatally hesitant. Pie was driving the Crosley, a gardener's mini-car, which had no business on a public road, but Pie had wanted to drive it. The Crosley was a toy, yet whatever Pie hit hobbled into the woods, dragging its broken parts.

Home again and in their beds, Pie and Nick took aspirin and turned away from each other and slept. Next morning—frictive love—and then as usual in the garden, Aunt Lucinda's garden, the famous one, a spilling-over, often photographed, sea-coast garden. The garden was how they lived for free. They were the caretakers in an estate called The Cottage. Some cottage! Why would Aunt

Lucinda leave this paradise they asked, but she had told them. His name was Bruno and his wealth exceeded hers. The villa he owned in Tuscany was staffed. "Everything here is arranged for my pleasure," so Aunt Lucinda said.

Gordon had said, "Scant pleasure." He had said, "I'll tell you pleasure. The killing kind." And then to most everyone at the Bay View bar, he described his wife: shoe-black hair and pointy parts. That cunt was the source of the fire, or so he had said at the Bay View. "I was fucking around," was what Gordon had said, "but who wouldn't?"

They were untested, Pie and Nick. They were newly everything; and now here they were caretakers for a summer before the rest of life began, and on this morning, as on so many mornings, the cloudless sky grew blue, then bluer. White chips of birds passed fast overhead, and the water was bright; they looked too long at its ceaseless signals and at noon they zombied to it. They let the water assault them until, cold and helpless, they let the waves knock them back to shore and up the beach. Sand caught in all the cracked places, and it felt good to take off their suits and finger it out. They lay directly on the sand; they dozed, they woke, they brushed themselves off. They wanted nothing. They were dry and their suits were dry and, for a moment, warm against them, and they walked to the shore; Nick and Pie walked along the shore and then into the water and they knew the water all over again. So went the afternoon in light—no clouds—whereas indoors was dark.

It was dark, but they ran through the mud room toward the

phone. They ran, and then they missed it. Who cared? They had the late afternoon before them.

They tended the garden. Nick and Pie, they watered the deep beds; they flourished arcs; they beaded hooded plants and cupped plants and frangible rues. They washed paths. The wet rock walls turned into gems. What a place this was! How could Aunt Lucinda's Bruno match it? Of course, the sunsets could be overlong if all they did was watch them, but they were distracted. The hot showers felt coarse against their sunburned skin and the lotion was cold. They put on pastel colors and saw their eyes in the mirror—another blue!

Another summer dusk, stunned by the sun's garish setting, they stood close to the grill and the radio's news. They were in love and could listen, horrified but untouched, to whatever the newscaster had to say. But the flamboyant infanticide accomplished with duct tape was too much. Just north of them it had happened in the next and poorest county.

"Turn that off!" Nick said, and Pie did.

For them, nothing more serious than the dark they finally sat in with plates on their laps and at their feet melted drinks that looked dirty.

"Death: will it be sudden and will we be smiling? Will we know ourselves and the life we have lived?"

"Don't even think such things!"

But Pie did, and Nick did, too.

He said, "Think of something else," and Pie came up with

Gordon.

Gordon at the ~~Bay View~~ Clam Box. His high color and his scribbled hair. The way he startled whenever they had swayed closer. Was he afraid he might be touched? But there were all those women. An actress they had heard of. A lot of other men's wives. Aunt Lucinda. "A beauty," was what he said of her. Cornelia Shelbey had been a girlfriend, too, until the Count swooped down. A prick, the Count. Cornelia Shelbey was a cunt.

"What are we?" they had asked.

"Conceited!"

Nevertheless, Gordon called them. The picnic was his idea. Midmorning and already hot, the coast, a scoured metal, stung their eyes. Even as they drove against the wind, they felt the heat. There was no shade for a picnic. The tablecloth, cornered with rocks, blew away. The champagne was wavy. The food they ate was salty or dry; no tastes to speak of. Nick wanted peanut butter and jelly on pink, damp bread. Instead here were cresses and colored crisps. Then the champagne began. Pie swallowed too much of an egg too fast and it hurt her throat.

Gordon said of Aunt Lucinda's Bruno, "The man's a fool. He knows nothing about art, but he lets people play with his money." Gordon picked at the knees of his loose khaki pants and what he found he flicked away in the seagrass. He asked, "How do you play with yours?"

They told him just how little they had.

"Too bad!" he said. "Poor you."

Pie washed her sticky hands in the cooler's melting ice. Gordon yawned. Then they all three pushed the picnic back into the basket, didn't bother to fold, drove home.

A storm the next day; the power thunked out. Nick and Pie still had a headache from the picnic—too much champagne and whatever they had drunk after—so they took more aspirin. They napped; they looked at the sky; they shared a joint, and they knocked around in bed and felt rubbed and eased when they were finished, and it was quiet in The Cottage except for the sound of the rain. They talked about money until they made themselves thirsty. Downstairs on the porch they saw Gordon in the garden under the tent of a golf umbrella.

Gordon said he'd walked all the way from the village to them, walked in the rain to get sober. "Last night," he said sadly. He shut the umbrella and sat on the porch with his head in his ruined hands.

So they lit the fat joint rolled against the threat of all-day rain, and Gordon was glad of it. "Yes," he said and inhaled deeply and exhaled in a noisy way, seeming satisfied, which was how they felt, too. Forgotten was the woozy picnic and the problems of money. After all Nick and Pie were a handsome couple, young and loved. Aunt Lucinda was rich even if they weren't. Hundreds of people had come to their wedding, and now they were caretakers to a scenic estate called The Cottage. The Cottage on Morgan Bay. For them the sky cleared and the sun came out and the garden began to sizzle. Gordon stayed on. He watched the happy couple, swatted by the waves: how they exhausted themselves until he was exhausted, too, and he slept. They all slept. They slept through the white hours of afternoon when the light was less complex. When they woke, the sand was peachy colored, and the sky was pretty. Gordon said he wanted to do something, but what? Why didn't they have any money!

They had the Crosley. "Fun," Pie said.

"Some fun," Nick said. "You killed some kind of animal in that toy."

Pie said, "I could bike to Gary's and see if he has any clams. We could have a clambake."

"Down here? After five? It's damp and cold and there's not as much beach."

"You come up with something why don't you."

"The lotion's hot. It can't feel good," Gordon said, but Pie said he was wrong.

"I'm so sunburned anything against my skin feels cool," she said.

Gordon wiped his hands on Pie's breasts. He said, "Lovely." He said, "Maybe you'll think of something to do. I'll call you."

A line they had heard before—had used themselves. I'll call you augured disappointment.

Nick's handsome face was crinkled. "What the fuck?" he said.

"What's this?" Pie asked.

"You're more ambitious" was what Nick finally said.

A cup of soup was dinner; the radio, left off.

"Find some music," Pie said and left Nick to wander through The Cottage. She swatted Aunt Lucinda's clothes until she found it: Valentino tap pants, and she tapped downstairs to nobody's music but her quavery own.

"The best you could do?" Pie asked.

"Look at you," he said.

On the beach, they agreed, their daydreaming was sometimes dangerous. The memory of Gordon's misanthropic breath against their faces came in gusts.

"Jesus," Pie said, remembering.

"What?"

The hollows of her body, especially at her hips were exciting to them both, and they smiled to see the sand running out of Nick's hand and into the ditched place between her hips.

"Jesus," Pie said.

"I was thinking I would lick."

Back to the garden, to the doused and swabbed, every morning, afternoon. Nick staked the droopers and Pie cut back. The heavy-headed mock orange, now past, Pie hacked at and hacked until the shorn shrub looked embarrassed.

"Poor thing," Nick said.

And Pie laughed. "I've turned the grandpa of the front walk into a kid."

Pie, a long girl, wobbly in heeled shoes, bowlegged, shifty—

bored, perhaps—but friendly, quick to laugh, on any errand making an impression. Nick left her on the village green the next afternoon, a lean girl in a ruffled bib. What was she wearing exactly? Something skimpy, faded, pink. She wore braids (again) or that was how Nick remembered her when he described Elizabeth Lathem Day—Pie was her father's invention. A girl, a pretty speck, a part of summer and passing through it.

She was. Pie was a white blonde, a blonde everywhere—it made Nick hard to think of her. She had close blonde fur between her legs. He liked to comb it with his fingers, pull a little bit. Fuck.

"Where the hell is she?" Nick couldn't help himself.

Lucinda said there was no family precedent; no one was mad that she knew of.

"Don't think we weren't getting along. Quite the opposite."

Dogs snuffed in the woods off leashes. Heavy yellow and black dogs, their rheumy eyes mournful, their hard tails always looked wet and swapped against the shrubs. Once the dogs barked; Nick heard though they were out of sight. Something they had found dead and offensive—not her, not Pie—Thank God! Although after the dogs, the reports, the calls, the case grew fainter.

Also, also Nick was drinking. He was forgetting he had this job. He found himself standing in front of open broom closets and cabinets, in front of the dishwasher and sinks. Sometimes his hands were wet.

. . .

Watering; he finished watering the wilted patches, then sat on the porch and worried his roughed-up hands, cut and dirty and uncared for, ugly as roots and clumsy. Hard even to phone, to push the buttons accurately, but he did and to his surprise Brisk answered, and said, "I'm only just home but I've heard. I'm sorry."

And that was that.

What was this guy all about was what Nick wanted to know. "Tell me," Nick said to Lucinda. Addresses, historic districts, the watch he wears, his antique truck, Gordon's conversation was an orange pricked with cloves—an aromatic keepsake of Episcopal Christmases; so it came as a surprise when he said he was a Jew. A Jew?

"You've not seen a lot of the world, Nick."

True, he hadn't. He had married young.

But Nick did not want to travel. He wanted to stay at The Cottage at least until spring, maybe through another summer. Who knew? Pie might come back.

Why would Gordon say more? Nick and Pie hadn't seen him since—when? That hot, flashy day Brisk discovered they only looked rich; they had money enough to get by. But how much was that? How much did it cost to get by pleasantly?

They were young, newly married. The most expensive things they bought were medicinal, recreational.

. . .

"You have no idea how happy we have been here," Nick said. This was the truth uttered later, after whatever had passed for dinner, after the bath that made him sweat, the third or fourth Scotch. "We were really, really happy."

The mothers and fathers—on both sides—made visits. They remarked on the garden and the ocean; they said no one would leave such a place voluntarily. So Nick stayed on at The Cottage. He watched the seasons redden then blue then brittle and brown the plants. The decline could be beautiful, but Nick's hands, ungloved, grew grotesque. A fungus buckled and yellowed his thumbnail. His hands, all rose-nicks and dirt, reminded him of Gordon's hands. Gordon talking about something to do with love, saying they had no idea, speaking in his seer-voice, the old, pocked, vacant voice, prophesizing horrors they could not imagine.

Not us. Pie thought and Nick thought, too; weren't they always harmonious after Gordon left? They said, "We're lucky." Together: "We are."

"You have no idea," Gordon had said another day on the beach. He had said to Nick, "Someday your mouth will bleed in your sleep, and her cunt, too, will stain whatever it touches."

"Love?"

Gordon in the buff on the beach that time, pulling at the bunched part between his legs, lifting up a purse of excitable skin. The black-haired, peaky creature called his wife had been a cunt.

Gordon had said, "I was on my way home when I saw the smoke. Up in smoke! My wife and some of my paintings." Gordon had asked, "You know what I tried to save, don't you?"

Nick had suspected it was not his wife.

But what was Nick doing to find his?

Why was it Gordon that Nick thought so much about when Gordon had shut up his house and gone somewhere south, southwest.

Oh, the summer! The summer felt next door despite the cold. Nick talked to anybody. He shut the place up. He was there after last call, at the bar, saying his good-byes at the Bay View, already shivering yet still polite.

Likable boy.

It was a dry cold, a snowless night, and Nick, so exposed in the Crosley, hurt driving into it. The starless sky was friendly, and the moon, if there was one, was wide.

THE WOMAN IN CHARGE OF SENSATION

DAWN RAFFEL

She asked me just to use the cloth in places in between again.

She used the word pearl.

The bruises were looked at professionally. This was not a fall, they said—not simply a fall, they said—but likely a condition. They were firm about this, and spoke as if in confidence, if not out of earshot.

"Can't you turn it down?" she said. Voices, a faucet. "The phone off the hook," she said. "Just pay attention."

On the floor the atomizer lay where she had dropped it, beading the plank.

"Careful where you step," she said. The room smelled expensive.

She gathered up pillows, in a strategy, apparently, to elevate herself—at least some of herself. She was ripping out something.

"Look at," she said. Things wadded inside her. Additional symptoms: Nostril, the works. She needed to flatten herself and pinch.

Balls of wool were on the throw. "It's crooked," she said.

There was more of her broken.

The experts were summoned, consulted, apprised. These were uninflicted damages. Everyone was compensated.

There amid the draped sheets; a slung arm, this, that—"I'd call it disagreeable," she said in concurrence. She tapped on the drip. "Prop me," she said. "Lift me a little. Pummel and plump," she said. "Go ahead and hit."

She had what she'd made, retrieved from the house. It was as she'd requested. Needles too.

They told her to make a fist and squeeze.

"What was the question?"—the woman in charge of sensation, a nurse. Marrow, cells, etcetera. A density ratio. "It works like this."

It was a button and such. "Easy," they said. "Easy does it with that."

I was not next of kin. There was no one who heard me.

They covered her later.

Salt was on her lip in there, and fluid leaking out of her. The odds were against this. It tasted like salt. I said it tasted like salt. There was no one who asked me.

It was I who dried her. I wrapped the thing around my neck, as she'd intended, arguably. I said the odds were against it.

The ankle was healing still, they said.

ALMANAC FOR FALLING DOWN THE STAIRS

JIBADE-KHALIL HUFFMAN

We see a sign that says "sell your house in nine days," with a number under the offer. We stare around this and over the sides of other things passing outside the window.

We sit in front of the window until buses begin passing on the street. The light is starting to arch over the tops of houses. Men in pajama bottoms and old T-shirts stand and look out of their garages into the beginning of the day. Women in robes turn and then turn back again to the water covering the street from the rain in the night and to the dew and the rainwater on the lawn. And they all turn again, the men in the garages and women on the porch steps and they almost spill the coffee out of their cups.

At the window then, it's my hands with her dress half pulled down and it's us looking out and up into the rest of the street. Her friend is dancing behind us. Her friend has these tall boots on and she has blood on her yellow dress. We keep asking her for cigarettes. We keep looking over at her then turning back to the window.

And when I pull her dress back up she grabs my face. Says she'd rather be going; that it's okay but she'd rather be going. She asks her friend for another cigarette; calls into the next room where the friend has backed onto a cot half tucked behind the door. A boy younger than us, Tommy, is laid out there on the cot, but from where we sit we can only see his feet from behind the doorway. The friend, Julie, is hugging at herself, knocking into things above Tommy on the cot. Pictures fall off the wall and books from the shelves. I pull her dress back up and it's as in all these scenes—the folding in around us of separate parts.

It's just as we stumble into the driveway, into the car, that the rain begins again. And it's just that we need more of what Tommy gave us, more of the day, the light sky up and around us and it's only the money we need to get to get it.

She starts up the car. She turns on the windshield wipers and we are looking at the garage door, motor running as we might run in place. She sets the windshield wipers on the lowest you can set them *and what a drag it is* that we cannot see a clear picture of the garage door in front of us. I slump near her as she pulls down and out of the driveway. In the middle of the street there are the yellow lane markers reflected in the window beside me, reflected in plural, the sound of the two continuous strips keeping us from the cars headed at us on the other side. When she puts both our windows down, most of the whole of the picture disappears, save for the now louder sound of the street outside. I hear this and she drives until she says she's found it, what she'd been looking for.

There's a car driving away from the house; it looks like a man's head and posture controlling the car in the driver's seat. She says she's seen this house more than a few times. Now the man's away, she says, and there's a screen door at the back we can try. She parks the car some houses away and we go around the block to the back and then over the fence.

In a modest way, we try the door and then drag it along the sliding frame a bit harder each time until it scrapes open. Inside the house there are at first only piles from the lives inside; magazines layered knee high, scattered spots of boxes blotting the carpet and facing out to us as we stand in the door.

Then it breaks away. The dining room table is plain and clean and the kitchen is plain. There are muddied shoes near the stairs but certainly the steps are clean. On the next floor I find the bathroom and she finds the master bedroom. She comes out with a few rings, a twenty-dollar bill cradling a few rings. She knows this house. Says she's watched it from her car, sitting on other mornings like this, staring at this house from a few spaces down the street. She smiles at me and we go into the smaller bedroom.

At first we see only the blood. Passed up on the wall. But then he looks at us. There are no windows in the room; he has this desk lamp on the floor by his feet. She goes over to the child and he starts screaming at her and when he pulls her down to him she says she doesn't know what it is she has to say to him what do you say to eleven twelve-year-old boys I don't know she doesn't know. As she says this it is as if he has everything, all the things in the room start to come down around them. The bedding and the clothes on the bed and the hangers and the posters off the wall and it comes down around him and her, the light bulb in the lamp crashing out.

We make the child walk a few steps ahead of us to the car and, standing on the sidewalk, we watch him get in. She forms reasons for him, pointing at his body behind the closed door; she forms obvious reasons for him. That the traits of the house are a sign of an even more astounding set of circumstances; that the ball in which he was curled on the floor was the perfect model for the sort of small instances of terror all around us. And I'm almost laughing as she says this about him, all the while facing me. She looks further in or rather more directly into my eyes and walks over to the other side of the car.

She and I keep repeating things we cannot account for later. We are in his house again, Tommy's house, in the living room. A warmer light moves through the room as the day turns to its middle part. She says she is eager to take the child back to his house—it's getting late we could tell a neighbor we found him wandering around here. We could drop him off in front of some sort of you know one of those safe or halfway houses we could call the father the mother and deliver an ultimatum a threat is that the right word I don't know. We could we could—she says she is both eager to take him away from here and keep him here.

We continue inventing wildly differing constructs. Going down the list. Ten-second scenes and draped monologues stapled to the same page with the picture we inhabit. Coupled with the words coming out of our mouths and the gestures shaping our bodies as they. As she keeps moving in close to grab me, say, by the face to let out a line of reasons but then moves back from me after what is revealed. I keep offering him things, bringing him orange soda and saying before he drinks, that maybe that's too much for you the sugar in that stuff I think I know I remember my mother wouldn't let me.

And this is certainly about particular strains of excitability. Tommy, as an example, and even the friend, Jane, stayed in the house when we called them out of the room the first time to go with us. And back once more, later with the child, though we knocked and screamed—as he sat watching us from the living room—they would not open the locked door. Would not even make a sound a peep to say "they were in there, but."

She left me at the house and drove him around the corner and let the child out to find his way home. We had finally gotten Tommy up; he gave us more of what he'd given us before. Then I told him I needed to dash around the room the light is getting lower in the day and I need to catch it. When she came back we sat and looked out the window again, until Tommy asked us to drive him to the store.

Sitting on a bench near the door of the market I see them go past us; see them stare in other places; the mothers and fathers with their children. See them bend into the wind and light around us. And look of stairs felled forward and with it, the saying on their faces; and I see them collide into the names, and the dates, and labels in front and in behind.

It's when you begin to articulate phrases about the landscape, the bare backyard and parquet floor that the world falls over you. It is up and away and then later you're again laid out in the back of her car. Asleep for some hours. Hung all over each other and other pictures and noises swing in around you. The feeling caked on your face of crowds surrounding, of the swarm, snap and exactitude of limbs and lips. The limp protests for the slowing down of it all. The brash and break, the wind and sound over all of it. With her face in front yours. Then nothing happens for hours.

And hours. Until we have to stare hard to see out in front of us; beginning in a child on a landing, in the swallow of the stairs, the walls, beginning with the day and the rest of the floor.

"EVERY TIME I SEE YOU PUNK, YOU'RE GONNA GET THE SAME"

JIBADE-KHALIL HUFFMAN

So small a picture that there may have been more to say alongside what he told; mouthed and screamed into his hand, into the breach —shows a gun at me, and says, "Every time I see you punk you're gonna get the same." And if it is here that we must enter the story, let us then suppose we have forgotten all but the *gist* of the beginning and are slowing down to a stop at the start of the center. As I am and as they were, *the main players*—though my figure in the narrative is sketched in its prominent fashion only through the forcing of the *I*—so I may and must and will begin with a general description of the two. Where we might otherwise find a start to the expanding description of the setting, we will find instead the fractured depiction of these two central figures—what they might have looked like, what they often wore, whom they most regularly quoted; a general list of their passions and most of what opposed these passions; whom they loved and then whom they loved. The specificity and length of these beginning arrangements shall vary and become—as a third character from out of the periphery once said—almost arbitrary in their degree of vagueness or certainty. The characters are: I, the I, writing down the lists and notes and quotes from out of a sustained glance up at the ceiling or onto the floor or into that corner where I just yesterday flung a jug of something or other—writing out of this lengthened stillness these very certain or to me certain-seeming points up the ladder—the top containing just beyond the rung a whole basket of other things stowed so as to be forgotten; the basket about to topple under the pull of what will have already passed.

This at first unfound manner of forgetting as the slapdash close to an episode or the end of a continuance or convergence of several episodes. An end to a scene or in this case several scenes that in their way apologize for the beginning—which we have skipped over, save for these descriptions of the three *heroes*—and save for the middle and for what led us up to the slow and then to the down and then to stop. As I am writing the lines in the morning of the winter, in January, in my room upstairs in my mother's apartment—or as I struck this to and away and about in the weeks that followed, atop a short chest of drawers in a clinic at which I was disposed of *by this very same mother*, or away from that room, while phone books glide at the door, as I scream that "they cannot say what it is I think they should say," and, "I cannot sit down any longer," and that "it is the same music that was taken away from me that forces my whole body against the door to be let out," and then into the same blind tune of silence back into my mother's apartment—as I am writing this down, several things will have happened or are going along right now or are about to happen. The opposing figure; the companion and friend as an amalgam of several figures from my, the "I"'s, past and present, who has brought herself to the edge or over the edge, as it were, into what we might realize as a sort of *epiphany* or *moment of clarity* —a *startling realization of the present state of things;* a long-approached digestion of what has happened that led to this realization; an understanding of what will unfold or what may unfold and loosen or slacken or run for the better or for the worse with this *clarity* in mind.

She stood at first away from me and I noticed this only after a friend pulled her over to be introduced. At a party, she stands by a lamp, looking out of a window into the spots of brightness dotting the night. Here I was with one of those figures from the periphery, the collective third character, on the couch, and when another of these peripheral characters brought her over to us, it was not to startle the narrative into a *crisis,* but rather to make clear the tone and circumstance of the character's arrival into these notes —that is, the notion of the arbitrary break in the proceedings of the narrative, the contrariness to which I lend this event to the reader and the necessity of leaving out or making absent what happened directly after this point in the narrative. The first event or crisis that followed, though it involved us both, had merely the threat of more than one car crashing, an *unavoidable feeling of sad-*

ness and a gun going for it. Here the character, the she, who would become the friend and companion, expounds on the virtues of my car as the car is pushed aside by another car into a ditch. She rubs her hand along the side of my face; the I here altogether afraid of the progression of the story. And to go along with the I and the she, several characters in the periphery worth mentioning only in their specific relation to the she and the I. The mother of the friend and companion as a symbol of a general sense of longing or the amalgam of her mother and my own as this. And soon after, the figure or the father, her father, waving a gun around the edge of my face, as though to say, there is more to say here, but anger states that I must more clearly threaten you, or rather, forecast an end to this by the mere implication of death.

Then follows, breaks, moves into the rest of the night, stumbles into a chair and makes into the room long rushes of hip into my lap—the friend and companion as momentary distraction to the narrator, folds her mouth into my mouth and pulls my arms around *these very same hips*—as if to point and say *Yes. Here.* To a feeling of long-warranted fulfillment, so as to draw a small arc in the progression of the narrative, a sameness in a field of broken-up scenes—*these very same hips.* When I saw her next, she was dolled up in a blue and brown dress, same as most occasions—as it is said in many volumes on the topic and in many articles and in many circles, regarding the idea of colors as symbols, that *the blue might imply devotion and purity and the brown humility and poverty*—and she said to me something, an actual *index* of things meant to parody that evening. Cars crash, boys run, try not to tell on each other even to save themselves, in descending order on the page; guns flag the scene. And I, then spurred, return to the previous pose, for *clarity*, the same picture from before. The I, as though afraid to do any more than stare away into the gray of the window; the blank space in her shoulders.

The day, the wind, sold in ends of stories; in early winter there on the Gulf and then somewhere *there's a score to be had*, again on everyone's broken sense of arousal at the previous part; in their heightened and dulled idea of who goes where and what goes next. The gesture of the start and end to a narrative; if we are to allow the story to turn off and into a ditch lined with shallow water, then once and for all it is here, in the winter on the Gulf that the curtain closes. Under boys dragged into the legs of picnic tables; swelled, black, muddy the road goes in brushing out the looks on their faces. In tall and round boys that sob and beat at their pillows of rest-stop-lane-lines, before more cars pull in; the headlights key up the gravel in their hair. They tell me to stay and that "you cannot even begin to understand how this would involve you," and "you were not even considered in the scene," or, "in the shoves of cars off the road."

To hear the *very same* rock band on the *very same* five rock radio stations set to memory in the stereo—as to dispel the narrator's attempt to affix a sense of repetition to these notes. And with this, "Oh to the collusion of several points beside the line; to the collusion of various lines," I say. With stilled and moving pictures of many persons, the feeling of calm induced in the manner in which this is told and here introduced and understood as a way around a digression or, perhaps, series of digressions; that is, to lend a more direct route to an end. That I can only remember the look of things—the indoor and out-of-doors pictures of surfaces and spaces. A second and balancing crisis to the predicament at the start of these notes concerns my being forced into a clinic *for youths dealing with various conflicts* and, at the swimming pool, her covering of her period with a towel and *then in the ending lines I take the keys again* and there are steep banks of road-ditch to get up from this time; there are windows to climb in where before she waited outside.

A GROSS

"Do you know where I'm going?"

JANE EYRE

DANIELLE DUTTON

I

It started out I was hungry and smaller than most. Not pretty, but passable. Rest easy, for it is not another story about a girl and her father; I never even knew mine. I read a lot early in life, and seriously craved love, but was accused of being a liar by my only known family and was sent away to learn to sell my soul to the Lord, and also to knit. Abandoned at school, I befriended an extraordinary girl who soon died like a martyr in a series of consumptive fits. Small but a natural watcher, I lived on through that season of death to learn to speak French and to draw. Eventually I wondered what existed beyond the fastened gate of my life. I wrote letters to newspapers and am so honest (not at all a lying sort) that I got myself a job in instruction and off I go. Up to this point I only had one pearl brooch. I had a black stuff dress. I might as well have been a Quaker!

II

At first much of my new life was what was missing from my old one, though still with chilly afternoons. I took long walks through generous woods and sometimes even on the roof to look at distant hills and (like all heroines ever dissatisfied) to imagine what might be past them. I have a certain amount of palpable self-distrust as well as matter-of-factness, but stand in possession of a heartily romantic imagination replete with the usual voids and sprites and turbulent seas. With said faculties in tow I wandered the prodigious house becoming especially fond of the third floor, which was almost as solitary as I am, and rather like a ghost. Sometimes I heard laughter, not mine.

Eventually the master of the house, thus far a stranger to me, returned to show himself. One might assume the entrance of a rich stranger with a heavy brow would be just the piquancy my story lacked; yet his demeanor didn't send me rushing down "boisterous channels" of love. Although I went on in the normal way—walking dim halls—I was altered and alarmed. He began in the meanwhile to summon me to his side nightly where I finally believed I could feel what I was born to do, feel, and be.

Yet perhaps I rush forth and relate too much, for he merely presented himself as a challenging conversationalist nights by the hearth as I calmly (or so he believed) worked on knitting. Some days he ignored me altogether. Yet, reader, I soon permitted myself to suspect he preferred my company to all other, even though I was small and poor. For I was considered by some to be almost a dwarf, although a pleasant one and rather with the air of a wood nymph. I thought: he wants to call me baby, but he is rich, melancholic, and much older than I.

So, to interrupt myself, I go to him and save his life one night and he grabs my wrist and almost does call me dearest and I say stupidly, "I'm glad I was awake." I should mention there was one maid who was terrible at her job and only extended the stench of her life outward to the whole house (or so I thought at the time). He went away on a journey after that and when he returned he was done with me and I with him, which is that part so easily overlooked by gossipmongers. Perhaps I exaggerate! We tried to ignore each other for a while is all. He was envious of my "heavy cloak of childhood," by which I mean my solitude. Apparently, he considered it composure. He wanted me to love him best and was even jealous of little girls. So he surrounds himself in a sea of shiny visitors to see if I'll drown on the shore with equipoise. He mocked me. Meanwhile, beneath my immovable hanging skirts he moved heavy breathing and hectic (of course he only dreamt about it). He saw the situation and he extended himself toward all the simultaneous possibilities for performance and concealment. He acted like a gypsy, a bride, a brooding dog, an eagle. Then he caught me on the other side of a door one evening and said, "I was in a room without light."

And it is done. It is love and it is (as he explained it) as though a string were tied from my lowest left rib to his and would, upon separation of too many miles or months, bring forth wrenching internal bleeding, or death. A friend at last! Still, I palpitate at the sound of his voice more when he is harsh than when he calls me lily-flower or fairy, for I am neither beautiful nor given to dancing. In truth he was all I longed to be—adored, well-traveled, masculine. He was so in love he wanted to outfit me like a tropical bird instead of the plain (but refreshingly straightforward) English sparrow I might better resemble. I was forced to flee. It's not that I am silly so much as I recognize the gravity of life most profoundly. Would you believe, reader, that the chestnut tree in the near wood I secretly held to symbolize our lovers' pact was cleft in two by a bolt of God's own lightning? Also, he was already matrimonially tied. That maid—in part—the stench wasn't hers but his wife's who was demented. My master had kept her in a hidden sickroom for years. I fled for the sake of heaven and nearly perished from hunger and from my startled heart.

III

What followed was eventful yet boring in a way related to impatience. You see, after I recovered from an illness to do with wandering the countryside as a diminutive beggarperson, I managed to befriend folk known as the salt of the earth and to paint a fine portrait of an angelic young lady. She was prettier than I to be sure, but I know who I am. I also opened a school, found long-lost family members, inherited a bundle of money, redecorated a country house, and learned two foreign languages. So you see, I discovered my independence in the purifying aspects of my pastoral hideout, for there is nothing like the English countryside as regards the edification of a dissipated soul. Then one of my newfound cousins asked me to entrust my life to his. Thankfully I had a mystical hallucinatory episode, and so fled, again.

At last I recovered my lost love in a damp valley. Poor suffering soul! He was blind, but I think blindness is a cause for astonishment, so I returned to my master. He whispered, "I see all our tortures absolved in fog." (His wife had jumped to her death off that very roof I once daydreamt upon!) We had babies, then, and traveled the world by train, and I saw foreign landscapes through clear and unadulterated glass.

PHOTOGRAPHS

BILL HAYWARD

At sites across the United States, I invite people to collaborate with me in creating their own historical markers for the twenty-first century. The words, the marks, and cut paper are created and executed by the subjects of these portraits.

The *American Memory Project* sites include Bunker Hill; Kennedy Space Center; Las Vegas, Nevada; Independence Hall; New Harmony, Indiana; Vietnam Veterans Memorial; Ellis Island; Gettysburg; Boston National Historical Park; Martin Luther King, Jr. National Historic Site; Selma, Alabama; Lowell National Historical Park; World Trade Center site; Women's Rights National Historical Park; sites along the Oregon Trail; various elementary and secondary schools; and Native American sites throughout the country.

Tom McKenna | Executive director of the Indiana Department of Commerce, New Harmony, Indiana

Susan Niles | College professor, Easton, Pennsylvania

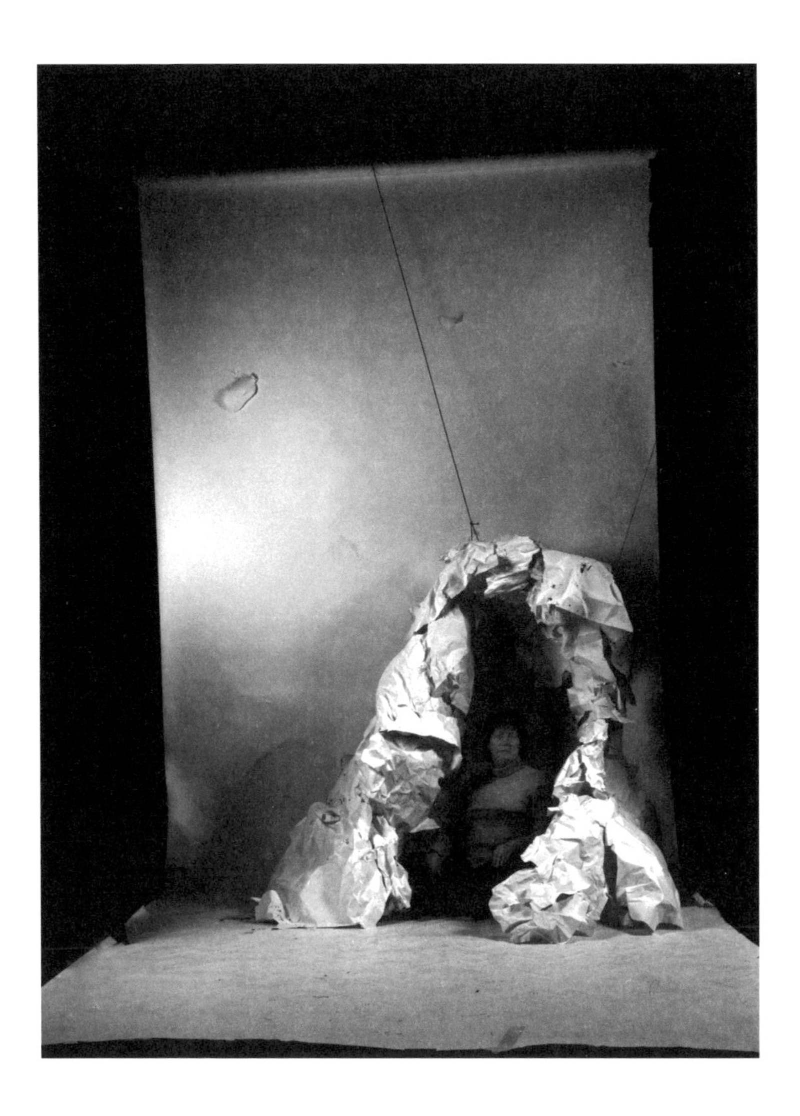

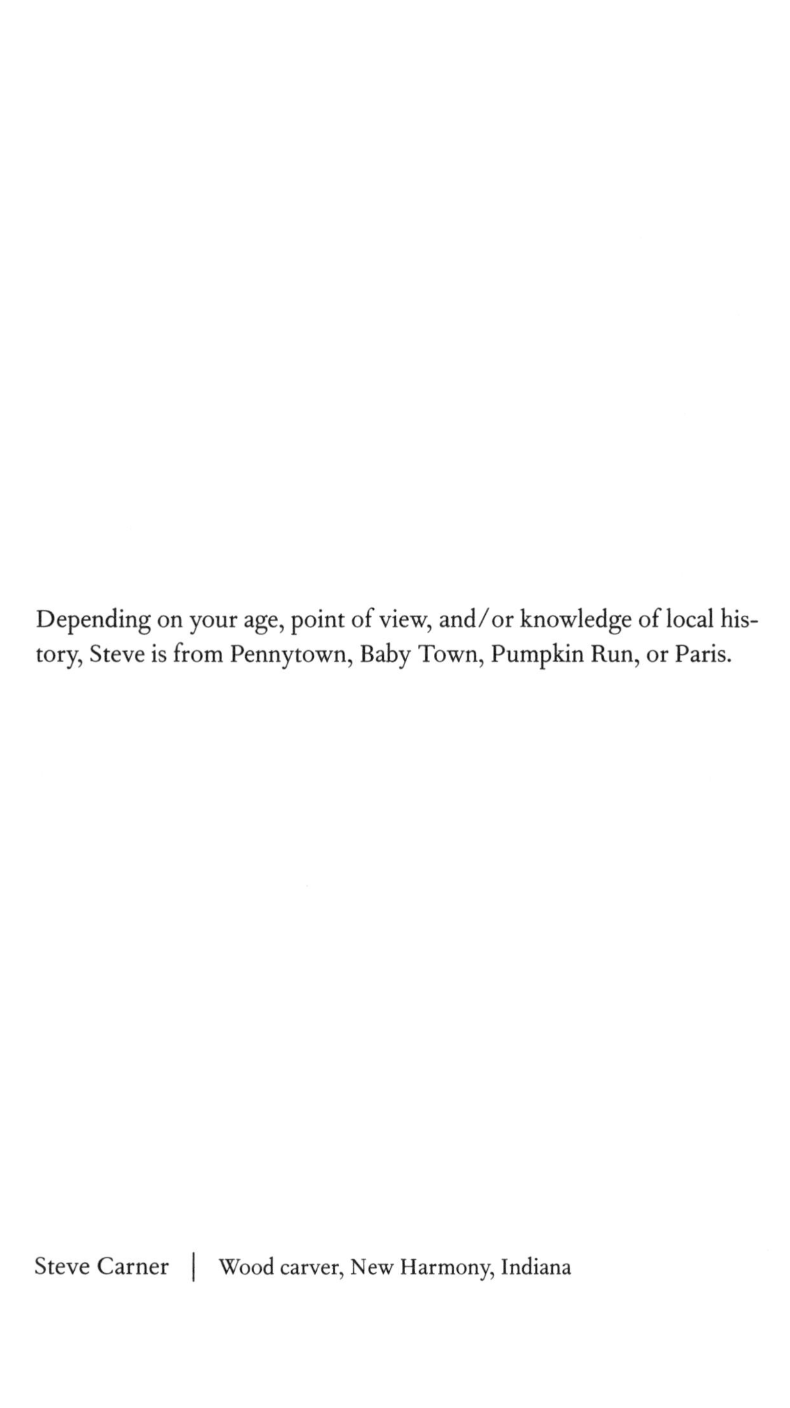

Depending on your age, point of view, and/or knowledge of local history, Steve is from Pennytown, Baby Town, Pumpkin Run, or Paris.

Steve Carner | Wood carver, New Harmony, Indiana

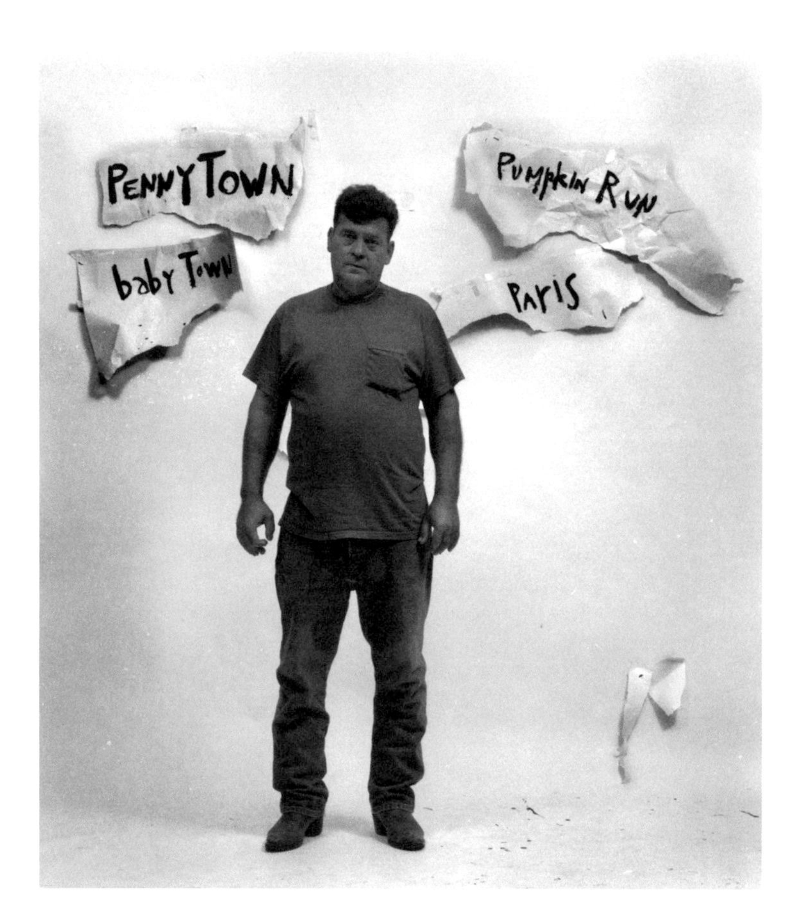
PENNY TOWN
baby Town
Pumpkin Run
Paris

"Depending on the year, I was born in Bugtown, Rapture, or Winfield."

In seventy two years in New Harmony:
farm hand
Illinois Central Railway worker
Farm Bureau Coop buyer
General Oil Field Supply worker—eighteen years
D. K. Parker Construction worker—twenty-seven years
school board member
township trustee

Ivan Alsop | Life-long resident, New Harmony, Indiana

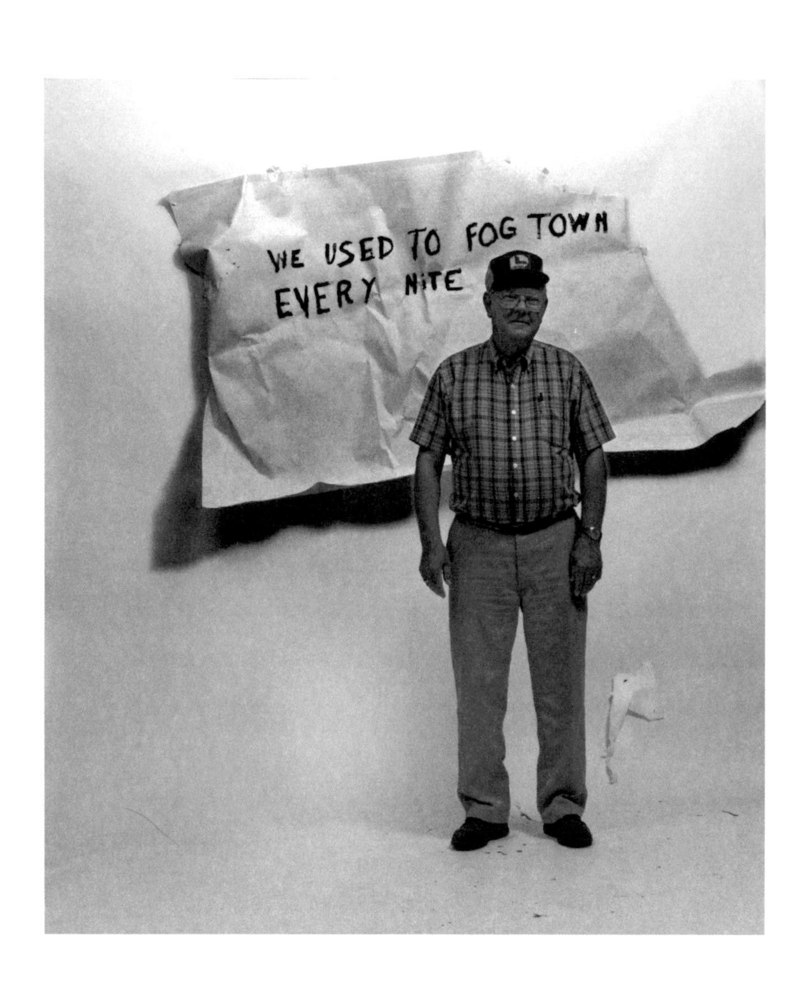
WE USED TO FOG TOWN
EVERY NITE

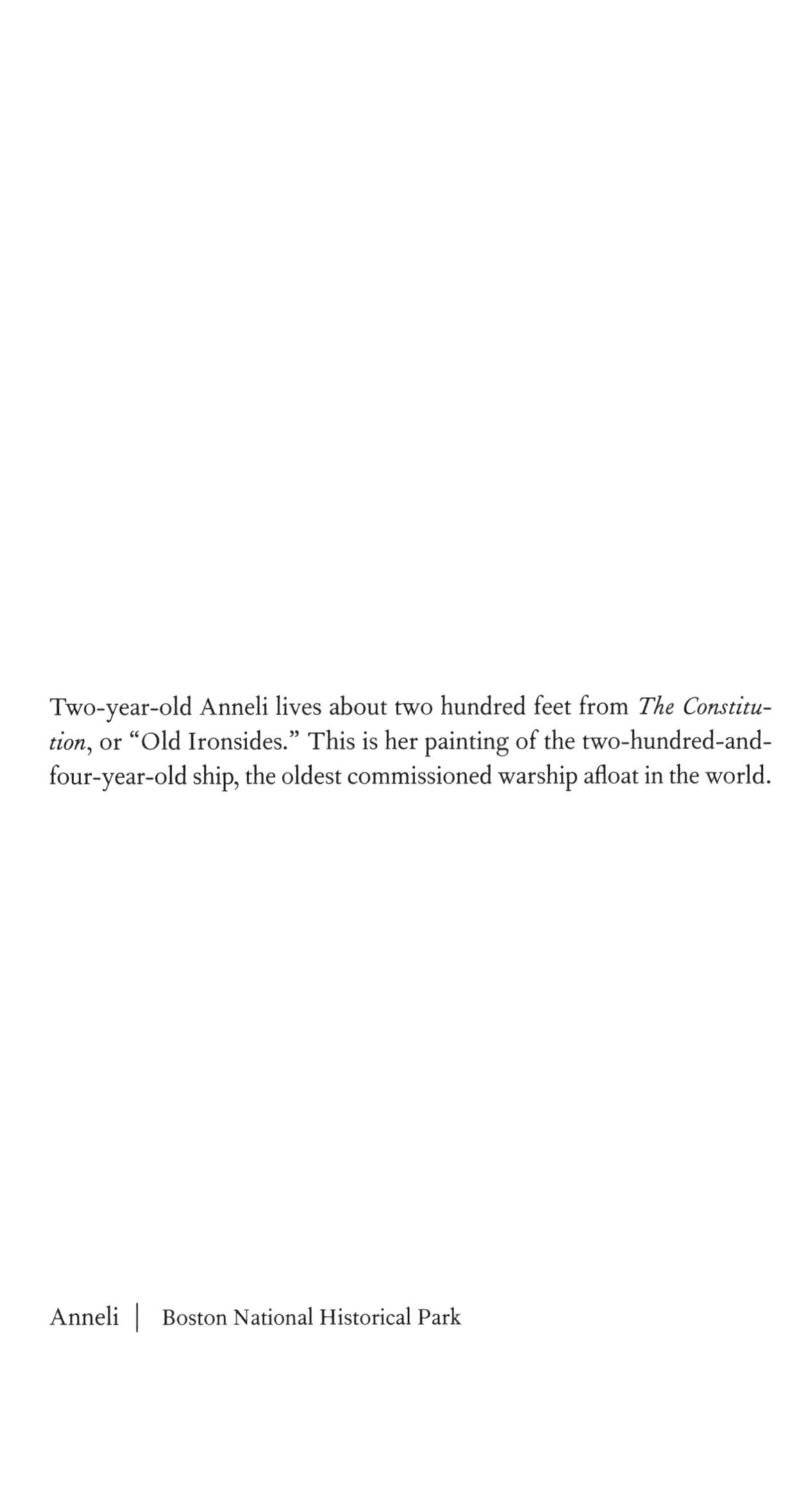

Two-year-old Anneli lives about two hundred feet from *The Constitution*, or "Old Ironsides." This is her painting of the two-hundred-and-four-year-old ship, the oldest commissioned warship afloat in the world.

Anneli | Boston National Historical Park

Jan Hitchcock | Tourist, Boston National Historical Park

The amazing thing about the American Revolution is – We got away with it!

In 1965 Alice M. West turned her home into a sanctuary that came to be known as the second Freedom House. Located in the projects of Selma, Alabama, West's home was next to Brown Chapel Church, the center of activity for the voting rights movement. West fed and housed "freedom fighters" and "outside agitators" who were welcome to come and go as needed. With only two bathrooms, five beds, and West's ten children underfoot, money and space were scarce, but West managed to keep everyone fed on what she describes as "common food." She is pictured with her typical shopping list from those hectic days. West's list includes: grits, eggs, biscuits, pancakes, peanut butter sandwiches, bologna, baked sweet potatoes, corn bread, dried peas and beans, Kool-Aid, collard greens, and neck bones. During this time, West remained active in voter registration; in 1965 she was responsible for registering over eight hundred people.

Alice M. West | Activist, Selma, Alabama

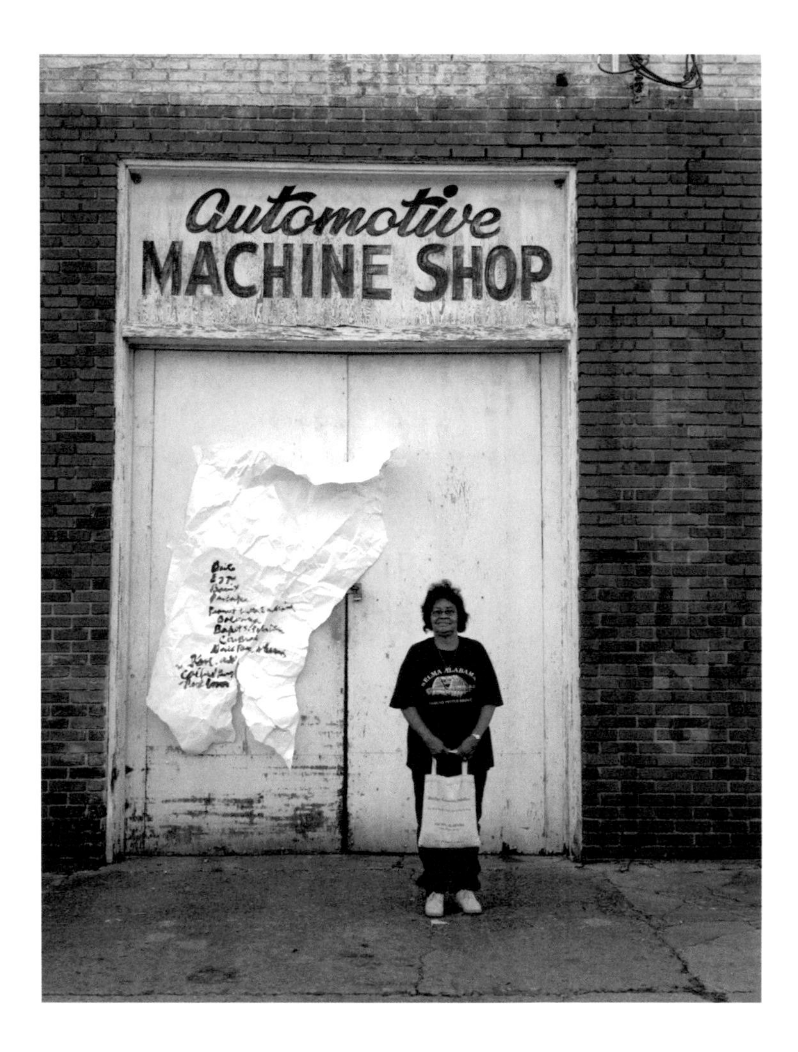
Automotive
MACHINE SHOP

John Manson | Supervisory park ranger, downtown district,
Boston National Historical Park

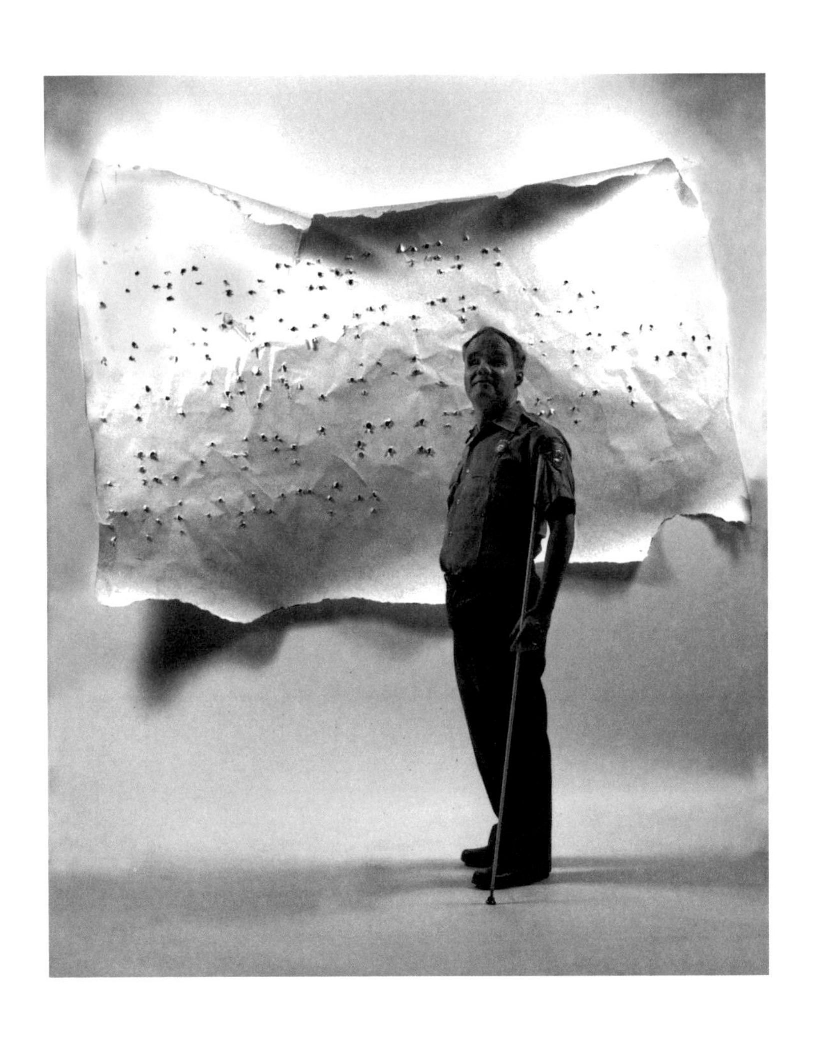

Nina | Eighth grade student, Taconic Hills Central School, Craryville, New York

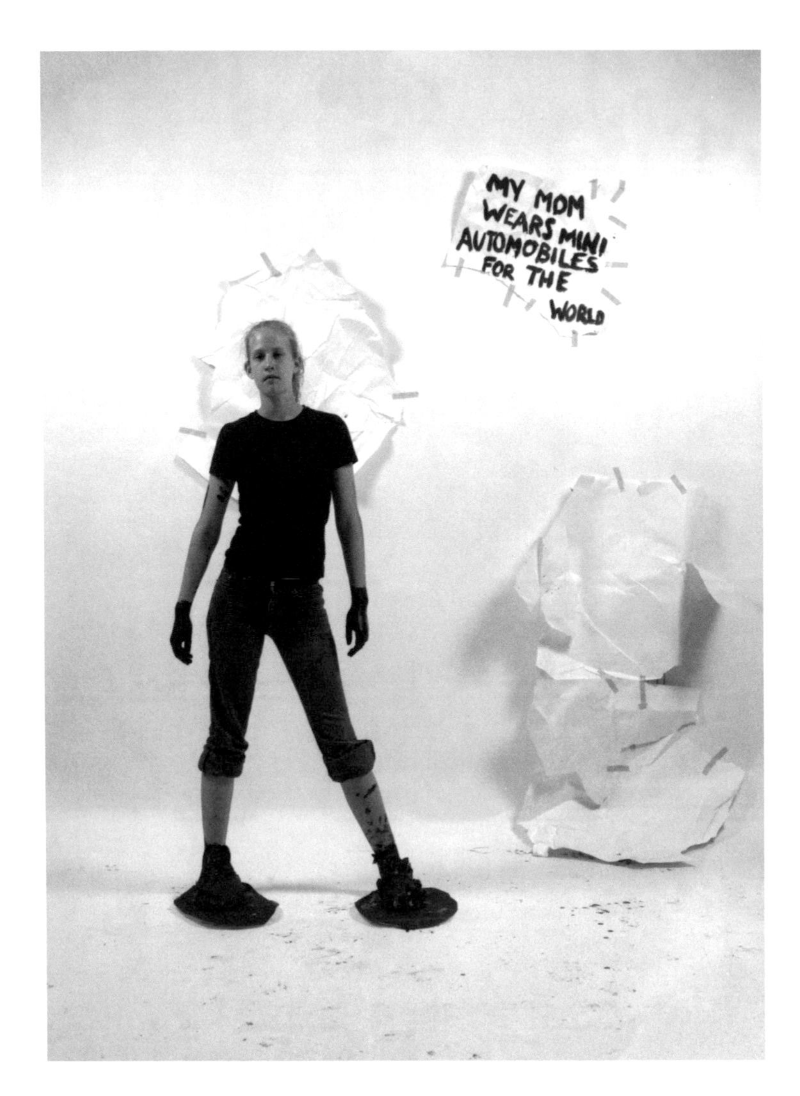
MY MOM
WEARS MINI
AUTOMOBILES
FOR THE
WORLD

PRETTY

KIM CHINQUEE

There were parades. I sat on my grandfather's float, wearing a red dress. I'd moved far away the year before. Now I was riding on a seat full of crunched-up tissue paper that was stapled to a box. I held a bouquet of artificial flowers and waved at everyone. My grandfather pulled the float behind his truck. I finally was fourteen.

I hadn't been back since moving far away. My parents had gotten a divorce. It was a small town of just a thousand people. My father had gone crazy, and people said my mom was mean for leaving him.

I rode on my grandfather's float almost every year. Last year, I stood, wearing a white dress, keeping balance, clinging to a life-size cross. I felt sort of like a star.

There would be fireworks. The boys had told me I was pretty.

I saw Jeremy standing in the crowd. They were all below me. I waved at him. He was dating a girl who had been my friend. We didn't talk much anymore. He'd taken me into the woods, and he was the first boy who ever kissed me. He put his hand up my buttoned shirt. We were sitting on a log.

I saw more people in the crowd. The float was moving slowly. My arm was getting tired. My face felt as if it were made of plaster, me smiling, my mouth open nice and wide. I saw the boys who I'd kissed in this guy Jason's bedroom. We used to go there after class, telling our parents not to pick us up, that we were staying after school. Jason was my second cousin.

In Jason's room, they all held me down. I don't remember much. Some boy said he wanted my virginity before I moved away. The first one who came inside me won a frigid six-pack. They didn't know that I'd already fucked my father.

I saw all of them, standing in a line, one after another. They looked really puzzled. I smiled. I waved to all the children. I threw away my kisses.

CELLS

KIM CHINQUEE

I was at the base's science fair. I was never good at science as a kid. Now I was twenty-one, and wore camouflage and combat boots. I set up a table in the small gymnasium, where I'd talk to kids about the elements of blood.

I was a medical technician, the job the Air Force gave me, since I'd gone in Open General. I'd made it through two years of training.

I loved looking at cells under the scope, round, some all smooth and curvy, yet some were granulated, some even looking square and bunched together. I marveled over the smallness of the platelets, at the way they gathered, like a huddle on a team. The machines ticked and sometimes made those whooshing sounds, and I could tell by hearing, and by seeing the robotic movements, what they were always doing. These small things worked together.

Kids were everywhere. I looked at the displays in the distance, devices I didn't know, atoms being built, a solar system with some kind of foreign rocket. My head had no room for them. I set up my posters about erythrocytes, and got out my needles and some tubes for demonstration.

The country was at war. We were in Biloxi.

I stood by my table, all excited to talk about the morphology of blood cells. Two girls walked up and asked what we did with all the blood when we were finished with the testing.

"Save it for a week," I said. "Then throw it away."

"Oh," the girl with pigtails said. She looked about eighth grade.

"In a biohazard pail."

"What if someone needs a lot of blood?" the one in glasses said.

"If a patient is low on blood, then, with the proper tests and orders, he gets transfused with a unit. Sometimes he needs two. Sometimes twenty-two. At times, there's not enough."

"My daddy's in the war," she said.

My husband was there too. I thought about the testing, the machine. I talked about serum properties, about the ph of urine. I mentioned properties and calculations.

I looked up, seeing the two girls. I stood still and very quiet, as if at attention.

BOOM BOX

KIM CHINQUEE

Last night I had a dream about a boom box. It played a salsa tune made into something hip-hop. It was loud and hurt my ears and it awoke me.

I was lying next to Daniel. His house was always cold, but his comforter was warm. I lay there for a while, thinking of the boom box, its beat still ringing in my ears. In reality, it was a song that Daniel had written for his nephew's seventh birthday, making it with everything he had, as if it were the only birthday. Yesterday, after he was finished, I listened to the song on Daniel's headphones. I listened to his favorites, songs that he had written. Now, after thirteen years of relying on the prospects of his music, he had a day job working with computers. I knew about regret. I sensed his disappointment.

Yesterday, he told me he wasn't giving up his fantasy of finding the right woman. He told me that he loved me. He also told me that I was not that woman.

After I awoke, I looked at the empty beer bottle sitting on the corner of the nightstand, next to my ticking golden watch, which my ex-husband bought the day after we were married. Yesterday, after Daniel mentioned soul mates, I told him I stopped believing in that kind of thing. I was skeptical of anything dreamy and romantic.

I turned over in the bed. When we slept, our bodies shaped together into one. He opened his eyes and readjusted. His skin was soft and warm and I felt him up against me. I didn't want to leave him. I thought about the dream, about the boom box. I wasn't the right woman. I wondered about the reality of soul mates. I pulled his arms around me. He put his hand up to my face and then he touched me. He told me that he loved me. He had such tidy fingers. He pressed them against the parts of me I do not name.

YELLOW TELEPHONE

KIM CHINQUEE

She stood in front of the classroom, writing on the blackboard. A tomato was embroidered on her sweater. She looked at the students who were eager, who asked a lot of questions.

Last night, she did shots of gin with her boyfriend at a bar called Yellow Telephone. He wanted to end their relationship, but he didn't have the courage.

There weren't any other questions. She wanted to feel needed. She liked it when they cared. A student in the front looked over at his watch. A dozen of them were looking out the window. Two students were sleeping in the corner. She didn't want to try too hard if she wasn't needed.

She was too tired to think about it much. Still, she asked them if they felt like paying her attention. Her students looked at her, staring at the tomato on her ordinary sweater.

TWO DOT

NOY HOLLAND

I had a spot of luck and felt lucky. I stuffed my cupboards with Ramen—fourteen for a buck. That was lucky.

I had a job I liked beside the rodeo grounds. I liked the bar between me and whoever. I liked the regulars. A bullrider came in regular and left me great wads of twenties. The old skinnies came in, little birds, to sing. Among them Edith.

Some people make you feel lucky. I bragged, "I have a bird dog who sleeps through the night all night. A sky light in all three rooms. Three rooms. All the lonely little feelings of the planet are mine."

"Not a care in the world," said Edith.

Nobody gets off. This wasn't news to me. Not so easy. I had it coming.

I tied jingle bells to my boots in the woods—to spook away

the moose, the bear. I stocked up. Pinched salt over my shoulder. Should I leave my three rooms, I left my lights on. I hooked my radio up to a timer. I was there, all right. I would be back soon.

I worked nights, regular, the sun slipping down. I biked with the sun on my back. I rode the wrong way with my hair loose with my hair in my mouth and eyes. I rode fast. I saw it coming. I saw the guy never look, not a glimpse, gunning out. Here it was.

I was cooked. I had a foot in the clamp.

We slapped together—my tiny force against his.

My bike folded, neat. A wheel kinked and collapsed, teeth of wire, a snag. A scrap of my skirt flew among them.

You pick up where you go.

I picked glass from my neck. Black nubs of gravel buckled my rump—a negative sky with stars.

I stood up—I stood up!—and kissed him—the man who never looked. I was grateful and overcome. He took it nicely.

I'd have a clear patch now, accordingly. A bargain. I could walk. I walked.

The road ran off up to Eureka, up to the sorry scraped-away slopes of the great blue felled Canuck timber.

They were waiting—my shriveled, tender flock.

"Late again?" my boss said.

"Late again, boss."

He raised an eye at me. I tossed an olive at his teeth. "Stick it," I said.

I got my rag out.

"Not again?" he asked. "You swear it?"

I tossed another. I took a swipe at the bar, and poured. Schnapps, schnapps, pass it along, creme de menthe, little dove, Drambuie.

I pulled a red beer for a rancher. Dumped his cigarette butts in the bin. For this, he offered to break my arm.

Phoo.

I'd have a night of it. Pretty bullriding days. The sweet bulby asses of cowpokes ahead. The bar between us. He couldn't touch me. Phoo.

"Try to touch me," I said.

My boss was watching.

I pulled the beer first. Next juice. I sloped the glass.

The trick is do it slow enough the juice runs in a grubby tongue. Slow. I thought: summer. The coiled hose; the spigot on. The hose flumpy and hot in my hand. It's half a mile away—the first little glub and sputter. Hey!

Here it's coming, kid!

What a feeling—the old jiggle and dip. The hose wags up fat and happy, *howdy*, running hot and clean.

The juice pools if it's fresh and clouds. His did not.

His was making pulpy globlets. His globlets were rising, lacy and curdled, up through the yellow wash.

He threw it at me, our rancher.

You can't smell it. You taste it and it tastes like can.

He offered to break my other arm. He kicked a mother beaver in the parking lot, going out, going home, back to the ranch, there goes a man.

The ladies liked him. He never looked twice. He thought he didn't have to.

They liked his high thick wavy head of soap opera chestnut hair. His truck with heat. His acres. He was safety. The ladies fell for him from age, the poor twits, a dull dwindling desperation. Nobody looked at them: they'd disappeared.

I'd be disappearing too.

I swiped at myself with my rag. I was wet. I tasted of can. My skirt clung to my rump. So what.

Pretty bullriding days. I poured, poured some more. I was in the clear. The big It girl. Deep in the Great I Am.

My girls tottered and twittered and drank, they were drunk. They were tired and weak and widowed. They went for creeps dead and living. The dead for they're easy to love.

They'd stuffed their cupboards with Ramen like mine. Tomato soup in cans. They kept coins, bills. Figuring. Edith kept hers in the deep freeze, sorted and stacked in an ice cream box. Frozen assets. She'd be cleaned out. She spun on her stool and bragged.

I watched my bullrider try to work her. Easy. He was young yet. He could ride the worst bull to the buzzer and walk. He wasn't marked yet.

I told Edith about my radio, timed, my lights I left on, she said, "Oh?" She said, "I am eighty-six years old as of now. Ever one of these teeth is mine own."

Her teeth were green from all she'd been drinking. Her lips stuck to her teeth. She looked ridiculous. Her lips flushed the blue of her hair, mis-dyed. Her face was violet, satiny as a banner.

She was at suck, looked like. Her jaw was popping. She was draining.

He heeled back on his stool, our bullrider. He looked away to let Edith fall. She fell hard to the floor and twitched there, riding the bits and spatter of her busted glass.

He looked away—too late, too much. Some tough. Our bullrider went down too. He passed out half upon her.

He took on the loose beauty of the fallen. His skin was polished—at rest perfected, his eyelashes heavy as a cow's. I knelt to kiss him. The others worked at Edith. It would be for me to revive him, mine to coddle him home.

She got her tongue down. A soft little gob of something cut loose and pushed through the slots of her brain.

"Do something," somebody said.

I took a swipe at myself. It wasn't me.

She was cooked. Poor poor. She had it coming.

My skirt stuck to my rump. He wore a buckle she liked. It was big enough to eat from. I said, "Edith."

It wasn't me.

Some days are better than others. Some people make you feel lucky. Edith was one of these.

FIBULA

GARY LUTZ

I used to visit a younger man in the big, voluminal city, the one that maddened itself out between twin rivers. He would call and say, "Just get here." I'd drive half a day to a town within two hours of the place, then park and ride a bus the rest of the way. There would be the rummaged abundance of his hair, the blooded trouble of his eyes, hands runted becomingly—but he always just wanted me to go out with him with his friends, a characterful alumni brigade. Once, one of them had found "the perfect winter bar," and it was in fact winter, forced-air heat had dried up all their faces, and my younger man returned from the barkeep with a timely femme fizz for me to spurn through a straw, some unobscured spirits for himself. Our table was two tables pushed together in unlevel, comradely enlargement. His friends were lounging quietly in whichever private, humble injuries could have then been current.

But my love for him must have been flush with the line of his arm as often as he got it propped up to make his point: that things should be kept figmentary on people, between people—

So I suppose, yes, we were serious about each other, only graver than two men usually are about failings they are fleeing.

Later, in his apartment, a walk-up, I watched him beat himself back from me again.

Before him, I had had a wife: a wife, true, who kept a glaze over everything. I'd have to scratch my way through it if I hoped to find anything unhypothetical. (She exhausted her hair with denigratory tints, and there was a tepid dark to her eyes. Contact was chancy, ungladdening.) It was a period, understand, of rationed, grating embraces, and then one day she came out with a baby, sprang it on me in a bassinet upstairs, and I know I must have eventually confused the thing with mock holidays, and lonesome toilet drills, and homemade cereals that just sank in the milk, and I know I must have stood the kid up in front of uncles and ball-rolling aunts, and then she vanished with it back into her vague-faced, waiting family. These were people who uprooted themselves tooth and nail, hurried their furniture over highways into ditchy, isolating towns. They were letter writers, but they mostly just wrote, "We know about you."

. . .

I have since turned many a corner in what I know of myself.

I can take apart a marriage, and sense when a possessiveness might be difficult to undo.

One morning I found a pill outside a neighbor's door. It was reason enough to have stooped some more. This was a petite, gray prescriptional with narrow digits sunken dimly into the face. I went back to my place and gave the thing a concerned chew, then put my system on alert for any improving diddling within. I waited half an hour, an hour, an hour and a half.

I was living in an apartment complex. There is no use in hearing the term "apartment complex" unless it is taken immediately to mean a syndrome, a fiesta of symptoms.

On the other side of my bathroom, someone was living a life that called for lots of water. I would almost always hear it streaming remedially into the tub, the sink.

People, co-workers, naturally inquired about whether I had a girlfriend, and if I mentioned somebody "now gone from this world," I did so in the expectancy that by "this world" they would understand me to have meant not the entire subcelestial estate or national agitation, but just my unlargening residential portion of it and the few places I might have once taken someone—the secondhand-clothing stores and bested restaurants of the unample town.

This town, you had to get your hands on a different, specialized map just to see it.

It was a hollowed-out dot of round-shouldered population. Roughnecks ran the college.

. . .

My younger man: He had moved around a lot on people. A lot of casework, social work, had gone into him. He lived on purified tap water and spangled baked goods. His face rarely carried an expression to term, but there was expression in his elbow, a mien to be made out in either of the underarms.

Some nights it was all I could do to keep from adding my lips to the mouth of a bottle he had once put his mouth around when pausing for effect in some gracing self-criticism.

His face? He called it a rat face.

His ass? He said there was a word in his grandparents' tongue for the way the flab seemed to be coming up from it in little bubbles. It was a pimpling or a pilling my dabbling eye had never minded.

There was a bar of soap he had used a couple of times, a woman's soap, with womanly incurvature. I had held on to it. I would draw it unwetted along my cheek, the distance of my arm. I would try to bring a little back, however much of him might still be sticking to the thing, because I understood the molecules of soap to be especially grasping and retentive, and the skin of a man to be not all that loyal to the body.

When you live in apartments, understand, you go over the communicating walls daily, carefully, fingering for sightways, cracks, exposures, scopes.

You awaken from a nap and expect to find something—television-sized rectangles, even—sawed out at last.

I was not a model rider of the bus, either. I saw arms, swaying legs, that might have belonged on anyone. Everybody was the same body, no matter the twists of personship, the agonied differences of fit and build.

Then I must have been caused to fall for a woman, a regular on the jumbly, cross-town run, because one day one part of her would be arisen, pivotal, summonsy, awag—a chancing hand, perhaps, or gleamed, unsecretful ankle. By the next day, the center of her would have shifted. A couple of public weeks like this, and finally she said, "So what do you think? Could you use a friend?"

(It's all about keeping any old hole as open as you can get it to go.)

I moved my things in. This woman turned out to have a daughter, a struggler, who was late to take after her. The girl's body was now in full, brutal pursuit of the mother's. The girl seized the mother's most liable features, brought them to semblant possession on herself.

The mother's face gave ground. I watched it unpile itself.

Her voice was a gurge.

I'd tread tenorlessly on floorboards on my way to the stairs.

Our life thereafter was jumpy and bare.

CONTRIBUTORS

Kim Chinquee's fiction has appeared in *NOON*, *Denver Quarterly*, *The South Carolina Review*, *The Arkansas Review*, *Confrontation*, *Cottonwood*, and other journals. She has completed a collection of short stories and is working on her second novel.

Lydia Davis is the author of four books of fiction, the latest of which is *Samuel Johnson Is Indignant* (McSweeney's). She is also the translator of the recent *Swann's Way*, by Marcel Proust, published by Viking.

Danielle Dutton's fiction has appeared or is forthcoming in *Fence*, *3rd bed*, *Pompom*, and *Denver Quarterly*.

Augusta Gross is a psychologist who formerly practiced in New York City, specializing in diagnostic testing and counseling of people with learning difficulties. These are her first published drawings.

Bill Hayward is a photographer who lives and works in New York City. The photographs featured are from *The American Memory Project*—a forthcoming book, film, and exhibition series. This project can be followed at theamericanmemoryproject.com.

Noy Holland's first book, *The Spectacle of the Body*, was published by Alfred A. Knopf, and was nominated for a National Book Award. Her short fiction has appeared in *The Quarterly*, *Conjunctions*, *Open City*, *Black Warrior Review*, *Ploughshares*, *Glimmer Train*, and other journals. She teaches in the MFA Program at the University of Massachusetts.

Jibade-Khalil Huffman's fiction and poetry have appeared in *NOON*, *Fence*, and (*Some from*) DIAGRAM: *A Print Anthology*. He is a first year student in the Creative Writing MFA program at Brown University.

Gary Lutz is the author of *Stories in the Worst Way* (Alfred A. Knopf; reissued by 3rd bed) and *I Looked Alive* (Black Square Editions/Four Walls Eight Windows).

Damien Ober lives in the state where his children were born. He sleeps half the year on a cot in his office at The East Coast Knife Factory and the other half in a small cabin north of Willow, Alaska.

Adam Phillips is a psychoanalyst in London. His most recent book is *Equals*, out from Basic Books. He is the series editor for Penguin Classics of the new Freud translations. "Begin with Temper" is his first published fiction.

Dawn Raffel is the author of a novel, *Carrying the Body* (Scribner), and a story collection, *In the Year of Long Division* (Alfred A. Knopf). She is at work on another collection.

Karl Roloff is studying theology at Harvard University. He has published before in *NOON* and has written a novel, *Shadow Boxing with Repugnance*.

Christine Schutt is the author of *Nightwork*, a collection of stories, and *Florida*, a novel just published by Northwestern University Press. Her stories have most recently appeared in *Post Road*, *SHADE*, and *Columbia*.

Deb Olin Unferth's work has appeared in *Harper's Magazine*, *Denver Quarterly*, *Literary Review*, *Colorado Review*, *NOON*, and other journals. She has just completed a collection of stories, *Mr. Simmons Takes a Prisoner*.

Christopher Williams lives and works in Los Angeles. He is represented by David Zwirner in New York and has exhibited extensively nationally and internationally.

THE EDITORS WISH TO THANK THE FOLLOWING INDIVIDUALS FOR THEIR GENEROUS SUPPORT OF NOON:

Anonymous

Anonymous

Francis and Prudence Beidler

Lisa Bornstein

Lawrie and Tony Dean

Joseph Glossberg

Ellen Kern

Laura S. Kirk

Clancy Martin

Thea and David Obstler

Abby S. Weintraub

Paul Williams

A NOTE ON THE TYPE

This book was set in Fournier, a typeface named for Pierre Simon Fournier, a celebrated type designer in eighteenth-century France. Fournier's type is considered transitional in that it drew its inspiration from the old style yet was ingeniously innovative, providing for an elegant yet legible appearance. For some time after his death in 1768, Fournier was remembered primarily as the author of a famous manual of typography and as a pioneer of the print system. However, in 1925 his reputation was enhanced when the Monotype Corporation of London revived Fournier's roman and italic.

Typeset by Matt Mayerchak, Needham, Massachusetts
Printed and bound in Iceland by Oddi Printing
Typography and cover design by Susan Carroll

Swoon

VICTORIA REDEL

"Victoria Redel has given us poems that sing from the 'full catastrophe' of a woman's life: erotic love and mother love swooning in the same book, often in the same poem! Poems of crucial friendships! Language as lucid as it is intoxicating! I'm amazed and grateful for this book. The world is richer because of it, and truer, and less lonely."
—Marie Howe

"*Swoon* is a startling sequence of poems—the voice fired with erotic hunger, the language sharply original, oddly tilted, and ruthless in its assertions of the awful and blessed truths. Victoria Redel speaks from the very spine of her experience. Open this book and she will pull you in."—Billy Collins

Paper $14.00

www.mississippireview.com

barking through the night